GW00762135

FIREPROOF

and other stories

Celeste Augé

Doire Press

First published in July, 2012.

Doire Press
Aille, Inverin
Co. Galway
www.doirepress.com

Editing: Lisa Frank & John Walsh
Cover design & layout: Lisa Frank
Cover image: *Simple Tribal Vectar Heart* © Pixally / Dreamstime.com
Author photo: Celeste Augé

Printed by Clódóirí CL
Indreabhán, Co. na Gaillimhe

ISBN 978-1-907682-13-1

The characters in this book are not your friend, your neighbour or your aunt, (or you), no matter how similar they may seem. People and events in this book are fictional, the products of the author's overworked imagination.

Published with the assistance of Galway County Council.

ACKNOWLEDGEMENTS

Thanks are due to the following publications in which some of these stories first appeared: 'Mammary World' in *Southword*; 'Touching Fences' in *Ropes Journal*; 'Telling Stories' in *Quiddity International Literary Journal*; 'Ghostgirl' in *Penduline;* and 'Molly Fawn' in *Pank Magazine*.

'The Good Boat' won the 2011 Cúirt Festival of Literature New Writing Prize for Fiction; 'DeeDee and the Sorrows' and 'Mammary World' have both won the Lonely Voice competition run by the Irish Writers' Centre. 'DeeDee and the Sorrows' was commended in the 2011 Seán ÓFaoláin Short Story Competition.

Many thanks also to the people who helped this batch of stories along the way, both writers and friends. And to everyone who helped this author along the way, much gratitude and good vibes (cheque's in the post).

The author gratefully acknowledges the support of a bursary from the Galway County Arts Office.

CONTENTS

FIREPROOF

1

Mary Phoenix Lebel. I got my middle name because I almost died before I was born. My mother says even a lack of the blood that should have fed me wouldn't keep me from the world.

When I got over my first word—*fuck*—I went around naming things: the *loomering*, *chewper*, *meemies*. The living room, sports bottle cap, nipples. Near-death before birth gives me the right to claim the world, name it.

In my first year of grade school—a year later than I should have started, my mother reluctant to push past my screams of *home home*—I could stand rod-straight, all three-and-a-half-feet-tall of me, and argue down my kindergarten teacher on my word for *each other*.

'Yourchother,' I would say.

'Each other,' Mrs. Budge would absentmindedly correct, her pudgy arms busy moving across the construction-paper-covered mound of her desk.

'Yourchother.'

'Hmm? No, each other, sweetie.'

'No! Your*other*.'

On the strongest days, I would fill with righteous outrage—*my* words, *my* world—and pee would stream down to the cuffs of my purple bell-bottoms. My mother was used to this kind of thing at home. 'Take after your father,' she'd mutter.

2

Eight years old, and words are getting slippery.

I stand in the kitchen at half-past six on a school night. I'm wearing my sky blue cardigan as I watch my mother put the oil pan on for frozen chips. Except everyone else in this small town on the north shore of Lake Huron says *six thirty. Sky blue sweater. French fries.*

I want to go to a sleepover at Tracy's house. 'But why can't I?'

'Because I don't know her parents and neither does your father and that's it.' My mother turns back to the chip pan. I mentally correct myself: French-fries pan. Except that doesn't sound right, either. My mother taught me how to speak, taught me to tell time before my Grade One teacher got around to it.

'But I'll be the only girl in the class who won't be there.'

'Don't be ridiculous.'

'But Mo-om—'

'Dún an doras.' she says to me, which is Irish for shut the door but she says it when she wants me to stop talking. She can't remember how to say 'shut up' in Irish. But her Irish words pop up every now and again. She named our mutt Gráinne, the Irish for Grace. She's to blame for half-past, cardigan, frozen chips. 'Now go get your jacket and your brollie and collect the post for me.'

'Mo-om,' I say, 'it's an *umbrella*.'

'Brollie, brollie, brollie,' she says over and over, smiling.

3

The first time we move is after the chip pan fire, to the next city over. I'm ten years old. *Homework. Dance. Boys.* We move from the Old Barn—transformed into ashes and brick chimney—to our brand new gold nylon shag carpeted trailer home. It doesn't need a thing added or fixed. It even came with its own yellow phone attached to the kitchen wall, to match the yellow fridge and the yellow stove.

Three weeks in my new grade school—it says Sacred Heart School above the door—my mother comes into the principal's office with me. The remedial teacher is there too.

'Hallo, how're you, it's a lovely day, isn't it,' my mother says, her mouth full of her usual marbles.

Mr Sokolowski has to ask her to repeat herself. My mother was born in a thatch cottage in the depths of County Mayo, and he can't keep up with her. So she puts on her speaking-slowly-to-an-infant voice for the rest of the conversation.

There was no more talk of speech therapy after that. Turns out I'm doing okay in school.

4

Twelve years old and I make everyone call me Phoenix. To my ears Mary sounds like someone who does her homework on time. Someone who wouldn't make stuff up.

It's Christmas Eve, and we're back at my Granddad's house for meat pies and no-brand grape pop and too much beer for my aunts and uncles. Except in this house they're *les tourtières* and *la bière* and when my cousins say 'pop' the p sounds completely different, as though they have almost forgotten to pronounce it, so it kind of pops out of their mouths in the middle of a jumble of French words. Even my father speaks French. It's the only time he does. He doesn't get drunk though, he doesn't want to get into an argument with my Granddad, who has no problem getting drunk.

I sit in the living room, trying to watch music videos—we don't have cable, so I've never seen the images to go with the songs before—while my cousins babble around me. Alain, who is home from college, says a few words in English to me. I'm running out of words, though.

The younger kids are blocking the television.

'Out of the way, I'm trying to watch that!' I'm met with blank stares. They haven't done enough English in school yet. Wait till they get to high school and they have to do all their courses through English.

5

I'm thirteen. Officially a teenager. I've already had my first kiss (in the shed with David Bourke while his friend Leo waited outside) and I've been using tampons for two years. Cotton jewels, I call them.

My mother and father have been fighting for a year now, the heat in every room intensifying. Flames shoot out of their mouths where words should be.

You never used to shout like that, sulk all the time, throw dishes around, sleep all weekend, wear the same clothes everyday, leave the dishes dirty, stay out till all hours. This is all your fault.

You becomes a bad word.

You used to take me dancing. You are lucky I was willing to marry you, lucky. You don't even know me, you never have. You don't know what it's like to always be a foreigner, a stranger trying to make this home.

I hide out in plain view on the couch, my nose in a book. They forget I'm there, and after a while, thanks to *Sweet Valley High* or Miss Marple or SE Hinton, I do too.

Finally, something ignites.

I arrive home from school, dawdle up the driveway. My mother is still on the phone.

'Where's Gráinne,' I say to the kitchen, the loomering, the

backyard.

'Where's Gráinne,' I say to my mother, forgetting that she's on the phone. She shushes me away.

An hour later she tells me that we'll be leaving this place soon. 'We're going home,' she says. And: 'Oh yeah, Gráinne's been re-homed already.'

I can't speak. My lungs keep on filling with air. I didn't get a chance to say goodbye.

My father stops talking. My mother is going anyway, with or without him. She's fed up of Northern Ontario, her in-laws, her husband. She's taking me with her, back to the West of Ireland, where there isn't minus twenty Celsius, foot-deep slush in May, mosquito swarms. My father gets left behind.

6

Thirteen and two-thirds. Words have shifted, this time in Ireland. At the convent school, I sit next to a girl called Neev (spelt Niamh, but I can't remember it if I picture it that way) at a double wooden desk. There's a hole in the top corner, and I figure out that it's for a jar of ink. How old are these? My uniform isn't right—I'm wearing my mother's white blouse, the one with the lace trim on the collar. And my skirt isn't made of wool, or even synthetic made to look like wool.

A girl asks for a rubber and I nearly fall off my narrow wooden bench. Wow, these Irish girls are advanced. Takes a few minutes before I realise she means my eraser.

Nobody here speaks an English I can understand. I watch *News for the Deaf* to find out what's going on. I get tired of asking people what they have said, tired of how stupid I seem after the third repetition. I smile when I can't understand what they say. Seem even more stupid.

Car park. Calm. I am unable to make my *aw's* into *aa's*. *Re-gawtta*. It will be three years before I can say it right. *Re-gaatta*.

I didn't realise I was Canadian until I moved to the West of Ireland.

I never felt like someone with a country before, never identified myself as one of that crowd.

7

I will be sixteen next month and I know that as soon as I open my mouth the hairdresser will assume I'm American. Abrasive, exotic, not quite as bright. My t's are still all wrong. *Artd. Matder.*

My father sometimes phones. I spend the entire twenty-minute conversation finishing his sentences for him. He speaks too slowly.

New vocabulary: *sha* and *sláinte*. But Irish sounds like a mouthful of mush—there are no common sounds with French or English, and I can't pick out any individual words, except for the odd *well* or *washing machine*. At school I'm exempt from the subject, so it doesn't matter. I sit in the library that smells like pencils, daydream about kissing and flying at night. Pretend to read.

Basic phrases *as Gaeilge*—shut the door, can I please go to the bathroom—fly over my head. Phwoosh.

I discover the power of vodka and seven-up out the back of the church.

Home is where your mother makes you live. Language is for getting by.

8

Seventeen. There's a fire in my belly whenever I whisper his name. *Enrique. Enrique Roig Castillo.* I roll my tongue around the *r*, buy a ticket to Madrid with the money my mother has saved up for my college registration fee. I'll send her back the money when I get a job.

I have new words for things: *amor* and *vida* and *lavar los platos* words. I lie about my age, my experience, change my name to María. It's less complicated that way. I teach English to children after they've done their homework. Their mothers call me *María Irlandesa*. I stand my full five feet tall.

9

Life becomes warmer, quieter. I am twenty-four. I'm with my third proper boyfriend, Rafael Almeda Cascajo. *Gustar, el poder, crear, en casa.* Like, power, create, home. I have just met my future mother-in-law. Her name is Teresa Cascajo Alvarez and she speaks a bit of English. *Loomering, chewper, meemies,* I teach her. Also heat, melancholy, tune. She calls me *el fuego,* Spanish for fire.

10

Thirty-one years on this planet. *Pañal, biberón, culpabilidad.* Nappy, bottle, guilt. My mother makes the two and a half hour flight, visits me for the first time since I moved to Spain. Juno is one week old. Juno Almeda Lebel. She doesn't cry much, and my mother takes her out in the buggy, *el cochecito para bebé,* all over Madrid. She can't get over the sunshine.

'Non-stop in January and nobody even mentions it,' my mother says. She doesn't know any Spanish.

11

New Years' Day. I'll be thirty-six tomorrow.

My daughter doesn't speak. This isn't how it was supposed to be. The doctors can't say why. By her fifth year, I give up looking for explanations, get used to the silent days with my family. Rafael and Juno are both too self-contained to reach with words. I start making up words, for myself. *Boogley-woogley,* the feeling of low aloneness you get when the people you love don't talk to you. *Waygondoe,* a slap on your own back when you've made it through a twelve hour shift teaching successive groups of executives how to say *invoice* and *quarterly returns* only to discover that your daughter has gotten hold of the matches at the childminder's again. *Zupe,* the little part of yourself that you keep on ice just in case. In case *whenever* and *ever after* finally come.

I move back to Ireland even though I can't get a job, drag Rafael over with me. He lands full-time contract work with a technology company. I snipe at him from the depths of unemployment, even though we're able to pay the rent. He smiles—infuriating—says, 'That's your Franco-Canadian side coming out.' I want to hit him up the side of the head with a frying pan.

Juno isn't ready for real school; two hours a day in the village Montessori is the best I can do.

My days are like this: clean up the breakfast dishes, vacuum, tidy, walk the empty hills, sort the washing, make lunch for Juno, clean up after Juno's lunch, nibble, wait, newspaper, wish we could afford to live in town, start the car ten minutes before I need to leave just in case it won't co-operate. Wait. Talk to myself. Try to remember who I am, living in the depths of Co Mayo, in my mother's damp family home.

Any days that aren't like that are spent in the hospital. My mother is in A&E again, waiting for a bed. Her lungs are burnt, the walls of them covered with black scars, even though she no longer smokes.

I am re-learning the old lingo. *Howya, half-past, grand, you never know.*

If you could see through the walls of our 1960s bungalow, you would see Juno sticking together Lego bricks, me talking my way through everything I do around the house. 'And this T-shirt needs to be folded, and you know your grandmother would have ironed everything in this pile, even your underpants', a running commentary day-long for my silent daughter. And I don't even glance at her at the end of every phrase anymore, I can hold myself back. Rafael reckons I talk for my own ears, that I'm the only one who can keep up with my need for words, for the shape of stories and invention.

My secret is that one day I know Juno is going to answer me, that she will open her mouth and all the words she has been keeping for herself will tumble out, and she will have tales from her world that I have only been able to imagine.

My secret is that I don't know how to love her when she stands in the middle of the living room, legs straight, back straight, head held straight up, and she points at the television and then at herself but won't look at me.

My secret is that I shouted at her over and over when she was two, the times I tried to teach her sign language because I thought maybe that would be her way to speak.

12

Midsummer's day. Juno has asked for a candle again. It's lunchtime, so I'll let her light one and watch it while she shovels down some mashed potatoes.

Our first week in my mother's old family home, the week Juno wouldn't stop shaking, I took her into town, to the cathedral. Each side of the nave held a metal frame full of candles. We lit every candle on one stand, and I said a silent prayer, a wish, even though I no longer believe in anything remotely religious.

The glow of those candles stays with me.

Rafael rings to say he'll be working late today, some project that's bungled. He can't say what time he'll be home, the contract is with an American firm and they're five hours behind. Dinner for two again.

The consultant phones to say he's not sure what my mother's treatment will be. He has to discuss it with colleagues, see what the optimum outcome could be. Words like *optimum* scare me.

Boogley-woogley, waygondoe, zupe, I repeat to myself as I drive home from the supermarket, unpack the shopping, mop up the apple juice Juno spills on the floor. Only one more hour until I can put her to bed. Low alone, pat on the back, wish.

No jobs for English-as-a-second-language teachers in the newspaper. Nothing in the classifieds that would even cover childcare. A smash, from down the hall. Juno is in the middle of her room—

her face tensed up so much that her eyes are closed—and she has her pillow in one hand, her toy hammer in the other. She spins around and around, scattering her night lamp, the monitor and her china money-bank all over the floor.

'Stop! Stop,' I shout, but I don't stop there, and I hear myself shout hateful words to my only child. My voice gets louder and I'm screaming and Juno is cowering at the end of her bed.

When my voice cracks, I see the tears streaking down her face. Time out. I lock myself in the bathroom even though I know I should be holding my daughter, whispering the words she needs, giving her the best parts of myself.

Ragged breaths, the cool porcelain of the base of the sink against my forehead, list out the street names of my childhood homes. I wait until my hands stop trembling and I can face her.

Juno. Juno, my baby.

I hand her a box of matches. An invitation.

'Not here, outside,' I say, and I grasp her hand, pull her along behind me, into shoes, jacket, up to Dan's house to borrow some turf. Her face is still blotchy from crying.

Dan has already set up a small mound of turf and sticks at the top of the low road, and he's happy enough to give me a bag of the stuff. Dusk is settling like smoke, midsummer's equal night setting in.

We walk about fifty metres down the road, me dragging the bag behind me, Juno holding onto her box of matches.

About five sods of turf, a couple of sticks. We form a small mound at the edge of the tarmac across from Enda's house. I hold out a taper I've made out of newspaper. Juno knows what to do; I don't need to say a word.

Enda comes to the door, wondering what's going on.

'Keep an eye on it, will you,' I call out to him, then set off down the road, another fifty metres, across from another house.

Another small mound of turf, taper, match. A knock at the neighbour's door, so they'll watch the fire.

Fifty metres down, and Juno is running ahead of me, standing in place, ready.

All the way down the low road, six small fires, maybe a half hour of flame if we're lucky.

After the last miniature bonfire is lit, I grasp Juno's hand, warm and tight, look at her small head bobbing halfway down from mine, wonder at this small self-contained miracle and how a box of matches, a fire, can make her happy.

Juno, my little queen of the gods, bringer of light. I allow my words to circulate beneath my solar plexus.

Smoke. Heat. Breathe.

TOUCHING FENCES

She's touching fences again. Careful to use her left hand, so she can still write with her right. Makes her feel alive, the feel of her muscles contracting, from the pads of her fingers right up through her tendons to tingle her bicep. Throwing her arm away. She grazes the live wire with the back of her hand, and then her hand won't grasp the wire when her muscles contract. She doesn't want full-on shock.

'Okay, now I can do it,' she says to no one.

The air picks up as she makes her way to the house, clambering down the pothole road to the neat security of streetlight rows and flat tarmac and identical houses. Unclaimed rubbish swirls around her, crisp packets lifted high into the air on an updraft.

Declan is cooking dinner, lamb curry by the smells that hit her the moment she opens the door. She often wonders if she dreamt him up, if one day he would go to the same place all her other creations had gone.

'Lamb curry, naan bread, basmati rice. Wine. All waiting for you,' he calls when the front door slams.

Fiona feels like heading right back out again. Since they moved in, she has been fighting the urge to bolt. She tries to say the right thing. 'Yeah, coming, I just have to do ... something.'

She ducks into their bedroom, weaving around the cardboard boxes she still hasn't unpacked. 'Don't have time,' she says over and over, when what she really means is 'couldn't be bothered', or sometimes 'I need to keep them all together, ready to go, just in case'. Declan doesn't push too hard, just keeps moving them into one corner, stacked up out of the way, so she has to pull them all down if she needs to find something.

They've been like this from the start. Declan adapting to whatever awkwardness Fiona placed in front of him, and she railing at his acceptance of her. 'But if it annoys you, why put up with it? Why not just come up with an excuse, a way out?'

She used to ask him this a lot in the early days. When they stayed with her family overnight, and her mother, descended into alcohol-fuelled conversation, insisted on leading a discussion on what makes for good sex. Brought up only to embarrass her. 'Why can't you be like normal people,' she'd hissed, unheard.

After dinner she loads the dishwasher, tries to act as if she cares about the house, their house, as if she's a regular woman. But she's just waiting until she can go back outside, until Declan is parked in front of Friday night TV and she is no longer needed.

She hasn't told him she's pregnant.

She doesn't know if she will.

The line still stretches between the rusted metal poles, blocking the cows' exit. The field is a depressing green, just tufts of well-chewed grass, no weeds or wildflowers to break the gloom. She has marvelled at these cows since she moved out here, a housing estate at the edge of town, the best they can afford. Declan hates the commute to work, the only thing she has ever heard him complain about. She loves the distance, loves the fact that she can walk fifty yards down the road and she is in small-farm land. Stone walls and black-and-white cows that look as though they could be cow models, they are such perfect specimens. She never thought cattle could be beautiful. They seem like her friends, they have become so familiar. Especially since the accident.

She didn't see the wreck, wasn't involved in any way. One day— out walking to get some space and a view of the city—the sole of her shoe crunched over broken glass. Bits of metal, screws and plastic casings still littered the verge. She couldn't tell if anyone had been injured. The wall had been flattened, a good ten feet of it. An electric fence spanned the gap left by the car. A fence was how she thought of it, even if it was only a piece of wire kept alive by a metal box tucked behind two stones. There to keep the cows in their place. Charged with 4500 volts so they would bounce right off it, only once if they learned quickly.

It isn't dark yet. Dusk is coming earlier each week, the summer starting to fade away. Fiona turns away from the lights sprinkling the cityscape below her, walking across to the fence. Relief—it's still there.

She allows the tension of anticipation to replace the anxiety that fills her. Her hand hovers above the wire, palm up. At this moment her mind is blank. Thoughts of Declan and work and houses and a baby and boxes are pushed out into the night air, there are no decisions to make and no one else to consider. Contact, her skin and a live wire, and she is jolted into herself, tendons and muscles in her left arm contracting.

The pain doesn't come till after, when she has to hold her arm gently against her body, so it won't get in the way. A dull ache that keeps her connected. Declan doesn't notice her distance, or if he does, he never lets on. 'Decide if you want to go away tomorrow. Just a day trip, to the coral beach, the two of us,' he says, as if it's that easy.

*

Echoes of her childhood self, the textures of her old world, filter back to her when she lets her guard down, while she is watching the ads on TV or putting away the dishes.

Fiona stands in the shadowy corner of the hallway on the night of her eighth birthday, listening to her mother shout at her father, when they think she is in bed. 'God damn you to hell, why don't you just go right back out that door, back to your work and your mates and let them wash your—'

She cannot hear what her father says to stop her mother mid-fuss. She worries more about the words she cannot hear than the ones that break through the painted pinewood door. The kitchen door moves an inch, and she huddles down, as if the smaller she can make herself the less likely she will get caught.

'I never wanted this,' her mother says in a loud voice, a shout controlled so well it becomes a threat. Fiona holds her breath, waits for the crash.

This is what she pictures is going on in the kitchen—her father standing close to the door, his arms folded over his narrow chest, feet planted so his weight can be born equally by both legs. Ready to make a run for it. Holding himself far enough away so anyone watching him will know he is untouchable. Her mother would be standing next to the kitchen sink, side-plates and blue mugs on the draining board since breakfast, in arm's reach.

During the small number of years she has been on this earth, Fiona has seen her mother do just about anything to grasp this man: shouting, throwing plates, making fun of his love of hostas and other difficult plants. Anything to get that charge of connection. Though he never threatens to leave, never once says he cannot take it anymore, he keeps himself apart, from both of them.

The smash never comes. She hears a dull thud and then the kitchen door surprises her by swinging open. Her father strides out, pauses halfway through the hall, on his way to the living room, back to his television. In that moment he looks straight at her and registers her crouching in the dim light. He does not chastise her, does not say a word. Picks up his step again, heads for the sofa. It is as if every motion and every stillness of his body says *I'll stay here, but you can't have me.*

*

'I only want to go as far as Rahoon,' she tells the bus driver when she climbs up the steps.

'Wherever you fancy, love. Just press the button,' he says as she pays.

Thank God he's one of the older ones, she thinks. Nobody needs to hear the details. Hello and thank-you will do.

Suzanne from HR wants to see her first thing. As if Monday mornings aren't bad enough, Human Resources would find a way to make them more miserable. Suzanne is the worst of them, full of enthusiasm and little ideas about how to make the staff happier. On the floor they joked vodka and red bull on tap would help. But that's what answering queries over the phone all day does to you.

The contact centre is relentless. On Fridays and bank holidays, the days most people try to do the least work, that's when customers decide to get on the phone and complain. Fiona likes working in the middle of such a buzz, the background murmur of agents handling calls, trying to sort each client out. A promotion came up, so she did the interview, thought she did okay. Didn't get it. She's too tired to mind.

So now she has to pretend she cares about why she didn't get the job. As though she wants to hear the specifics.

'Now in the interview, you didn't do so bad ...'

Fiona drifts out of the small room, into her imagination. She pictures the cows chewing in the field, slips inside one. Tries on a cow life. It doesn't seem that different to hers. Just less choice. A good thing, right now.

'... and where you really let yourself down was the psychometric testing, Fiona.'

Jolted back by the sound of her name, she tries to say something sensible. 'Um, I've never done one before—'

'Yes, now, to be honest with you, with these results, you're lucky you've got the job you're in. You'd want to talk this over with your supervisor, see if you can improve your productivity, Fiona.' She pauses, allows Fiona to justify herself.

'But have there been any complaints about me? I do my job. I do it well. How could it all depend on what a test says?'

'Well, you should have modified your behaviour till it became unconscious, so it would show up on a psychometric test.'

Fiona likes that idea, that you could have that much control over your own personality, you could mould a new one. She stands when Suzanne starts to get out of her chair. 'Thanks,' she says, when what she really wanted to say was 'you stupid bitch, who the hell let you work with other people?'

Work is easy. More room for saying things that don't matter. Someone always waiting to tell you what to do.

She thinks of the first thrill she felt right up the length of her spine, from her tailbone to the nape of her neck, an idea Fiona had laughed at when she first read about it. A raw fourteen years of age and suddenly she wakes up from whatever slumber has kept her under the surface, and she sees the world she has been walking around in for over a decade, sees it clearly, how all the outlines push against each other, as if she has never looked around herself before.

His name is Mark, and she studies the way his hair is sun-bleached, the lock that licks up over his forehead and how soft it looks, how his lips are fuller than a boy's should be. He is at least two inches taller than her, a critical gap that she has failed to notice before. Fiona takes to watching him whenever he and his friends call over to one of her neighbours, sauntering up the street as if he knows she is absorbing each step. And as clear as if she has spoken the words out loud, she hears: *you are going to stand close to that boy, whatever happens, and you are going to kiss him.*

In the quiet of her bedroom, she loves to say his name out loud, as though each motion of her lips over that one syllable is a kiss. She wonders how she never noticed the way her belly and thighs could burn with just a thought, and bides her time until she will see Mark again.

The summer passes faster than a sun shower. Mark never looks up, never sees the shadow in the bedroom window that Fiona is fleshing out, fashioning into the girl who will get away.

When she gets home, Declan is already there. She walks in the front door, touches the boxes perched against one wall of the hallway. Touches Declan when she enters the kitchen, just a brush of fingertips against his upper arm. She is not sure he notices. Rubs her palm along her belly, low down, without thinking.

'You ever just wish someone would tell you all the right choices, would just line you up in front of the right door, give you a nudge?' The words are out before she wants them to be.

Declan is sorting through the pantry, figuring out what they need at the supermarket. He likes to stock up. Shelves disappear under his food clutter: two kinds of oil—rapeseed and extra virgin olive, ketchup, Worcestershire sauce, shallots and onions, garlic, basmati rice, salt, dark soy sauce, bay leaves, basil, chilli powder, dark muscovado sugar, twelve-year-old Jameson, easy-cook lasagne sheets, tins of corn, baked beans and chick peas, a bag of cornflour, three packets of raspberry jelly powder.

He shakes his head. 'I like being surprised. And I like what happens when I choose well.' He looks at her, an intensity in his eyes, as if they're doing the talking. She knows he loves her. More than she loves him.

Fiona tries to remember the gust of wind that brought her here, to this life with Declan. She picks on one day, a few months after they met, narrows it down to the hour, then smaller.

The moment they walked into the living room of her rented flat, the flat she shared with two English language students—that's when it happened, when what they had became a relationship, a separate entity to them both, pulling them together, redefining their edges. When Fiona thinks of it, she still shivers.

Not a word passes between them as they sit down on either end of the sagging grey couch, not one word for fifteen minutes, not even a touch. She can feel Declan's presence in the room, as though she has grown a different kind of skin, sensitive to the thought of his hands. And she settles into this new skin, this silence that touches them both, joins them in this musty room. Comfort slips in under her breastbone, a secret, and she knows this feeling will stay when he carefully slices into the silence as though it is a tower of sponge cake and says, 'Toast. You can't beat a slice of warm toast with the butter dripping off it on a wet day like today.'

His undercurrent of humour gets to her, as if he can move past any obstacle, step right over sick bosses and moody puppies and make rear-ending the car in front of you seem as if it happened just to liven up the day. From these fifteen minutes in her front room, she thinks maybe he could take her with him, or at least show her how he manages this trick of perception.

Later, she will try to pinpoint the moment she herself becomes an obstacle, intractable in her habits and her moods.

Sneaking out is getting tougher. Declan wants to know where she's going now. Will she be long. So she pretends to need something from the car and walks up the road as fast as her feet will go. She needs to feel it. Needs the surge.

Fiona thinks about going over to London, flying over for a pretend shopping trip, getting rid of the baby. But she can't decide. Wouldn't be able to pack, even if she wanted to. So she follows her feet, lets them take her back up to the cows.

'What's the right thing to do?' she asks them. 'What should I do?'

They watch her, wide-eyed and steady, till she feels as though she's the one behind the fence. She drops her gaze to the wire, raises her left hand, the one she should be using. It's the one she started using, the one her mother held onto so she could learn to use her right hand. So she could be like the other girls. So it would be easier for her.

Baby, Declan, her job. Different roles, different demands, different drains on her. What to do?

Then there's the fence.

Stop, enough. She doesn't know, she simply doesn't know.

Her hand steadies as she anticipates her muscles tightening, the ache that will take her through the night, a sensation for tomorrow. Pushing all thought out so she is surprised by the bubbles that rise from her pelvis, as though she has moved into another body. A moment of stillness, then the bubbling returns, like unwelcome wind. Insistent, making her body respond. Excitement wells up in her solar plexus while she tries to push down with her mind—*you don't want this!*

The bubbling stills, then returns, rising over and over until she lets her hand graze the fence. The ache is instant.

She rests that hand on her belly, gives a sad look to the cows.

'Goodbye,' she calls to them.

MOLLY FAWN

Things you (probably) shouldn't tell your boyfriend:

That you once exchanged a backseat fuck for money. But it was only one of the Byrne brothers, from down the road in Glasnevin.

That your mother lives in a mental institution—St Brendan's over in Grangegorman.

That you prefer doodling pictures on the backs of scrap envelopes to doing anything else (except maybe sleeping) and that includes talking, making love and spending time with him.

That you didn't realise it was going to take you this long to wake up from the moment you pricked your finger on the needle of the orange portable record player down in George's Street Arcade. That when he stepped out from behind the sandwich stall to give you a blue plaster that looked like electrical tape, you didn't picture yourself living with him three years later. That if you had known this at the time, you might not have said yes to lunch in Stephen's Green.

That you can't face another night out with his friends, talking about last night's episode of *CSI* while secretly wondering if that beauty spot on the side of his face is cancerous.

That you dropped out of college because you developed an intense relationship with the colour red. You painted everything red, modelled sculptures out of red plasticine, refused to do colour studies based on any other pigment and ended up developing an intense relationship with your printmaking lecturer so it got to the point where his class was the only class you weren't failing.

That your friend Sinéad who lived next door to you during the grey years of secondary school when your mother could just about keep it together (as long as you got the groceries, cooked dinner, nagged her to pay the ESB bill so it wouldn't get cut off again, screened phone calls so she wouldn't get any bad news) is the only person you trust with the knowledge that you once had a crush on Lois Lane.

That it isn't you, it's him: his only hobby is staying home to smoke his brains to the ceiling and for a thirty-year-old he spends far too much time ringing his mother for advice. Plus, you're not sure you can listen to one more tale of what-we-did-at-the-stall-today.

That you only took the job on Arnott's beauty counter for the free makeup and samples. That and the fact that you've recently discovered black, and when the counter is quiet you enjoy painting small tattoos on your arm using liquid eyeliner that you cover up when your manager is around.

That when you get old you want to be like the red-lipstick lady who comes in to buy Yves Saint Laurent *Red Taboo*, with her hair sculptured around her head, loud scarves that clash with her outfit, and high-heels (even though she must be seventy). The kind of lady who could swear like a sailor while smiling.

That the time you texted him *Too love to stay Good room*, you really meant to text *Too loud to stay Home soon*, but your predictive text put in the wrong words and you only noticed the second you hit send.

That your manager is grooming you as her replacement while she's on maternity leave but you think you're not ready for the responsibility and you're worried if you take over her job you might end up with her life.

That you're bored of wearing stonewash jeans and desert boots. That you wished you looked cool, or at least interesting. Fawn-coloured, your first boyfriend once said. A fancy word for beige.

That a guy who looks like he got stuck at age sixteen bought eyeliner from you, spotted your ornate arm doodle, and asked you if you would like to do make-up for the New Duffy's Circus. That you told him you would except you don't approve of transporting animals around the country for the gratification of humans and he said in this circus only the humans wear chains.

That you don't look average or boring in any way once you're dressed up in a skin-tight PVC dress.

That when you told him you loved him you actually meant you loved having him around but you were afraid if you didn't say it back he would think you weren't serious about him.

That the reason you were home late is you were helping Guy put up circus posters in the city centre, on the hoardings in front of abandoned building sites, in head shops and chemists, on the notice boards of the libraries along the walk home.

That Guy gave you a free ticket and when you watch the acrobats fly past the top of the old circus tent you can imagine yourself doing anything in this city, even the world.

That you're a moonstone, picking up whatever emotional shifts waft around you, changing your colours to suit the person you're with. That you were never really in love with him; you were just trying him out. That you're only twenty-two and he's not the last older man you'll go out with.

That Guy came back again and asked if you want to hit the road for the summer, help out with costumes and make-up. That even though you think he's gay, you think you might say yes.

That you believe the right way to do things is backwards and that's why now that you are breaking up with him you will kiss him without thinking of anyone else and fall right in love with the smell of his skin and the way his hand feels on the small of your back.

That you don't know what you're doing or where you're going but you like the idea of travelling around your own country as a stranger. Even the small towns and villages sound exotic: Boris-on-Ossory, Kill, Mooncoin. That there are towns the world over that need the distraction of small circuses, of tight-rope walkers and she-male baritone ringmasters, and women who can flip mid-air to grasp a bar that has swung from the other side of the tent.

That you don't think you'll ever know where you're going, you've got too much to leave behind.

MAMMARY WORLD

I consider lying to my mother about why I got the job in Supervalu, giving her what she expects to hear. All the other girls are doing it. How else can I buy the small stuff? But I want to piss off my mother, so I go with the truth. 'I'm saving up for a boob job. A reduction.'

She gets that frozen face, clams her mouth shut, looks at me. I hate the silent treatment, she's too good at it. But I'm not budging on this one. *The Irish Mail on Sunday* did a special feature on breast reductions a few months ago. I sleep with the folded-up newspaper page under my pillow.

Walking up the village's biggest hill to the supermarket is the hardest part of my new job. The rest of it is okay, same rules as school. No iPods, no mobile phones, no chewing gum. Don't 'borrow' the stock. Don't sign into the till on someone else's name. Clock in when you get here, clock out when you leave. I like that no one checks up on me, that I can take my break with Nora, who smokes five cigarettes in a row behind the stockroom doors and tells us what her neighbours are up to. Mr O'Connor—Mike, I'm supposed to call him—said he would take me on because I didn't look like hassle. Then he looked right at me, as if he could see what was going on inside me, as if he knew me better than I ever could.

'Any problems, let me know. Nora will show you the till,' he said and walked back to the door that led down to the stockroom and his office.

'He doesn't come out front if he can help it,' Nora said in a low voice, the kind that older women use when they think someone might be listening. 'Customers are *our* problem.'

At nine o'clock on a Monday morning there aren't many customers.

Bikini Goddess stares at me all morning long, watching every little fumble I make with customers' change. She's made of cardboard and she stands next to the special-offer suntan lotion. She has a perfect fake tan and the exact right-sized breasts—not so big they hang down and make her look fat, not so small you wouldn't look at them first. And she smiles the whole time, while people stare at them.

I try to make time move faster by imagining what she is thinking. *Yellow is my absolute favourite colour, I love it so much I have ten bikinis in shades of yellow from pale lemon to sunflower gold. If only I could wiggle my left toe I could hop right out of this blue sky world and whirl across your vinyl floor. And really, my mouth hurts with all this phoney happiness, the drugs don't even work anymore.*

The past three years, I too have learnt the art of the blank face. Whenever I catch another man slide his eyes from my F-cups to the rest of me, I freeze the outside of myself. This time it's one of the neighbours.

'Here's your change, Padraig.'

'Great girl. You're a great girl, Tricia.' All said to my chest.

'Only one more hour to go,' Nora hollers across the aisle. She's at the express checkout, re-stocking chocolate bars and mints. I've discovered that Nora only has two settings, whisper and deafening, and that she lives for cigarette breaks. For her part, Nora has already found out that my parents are the Mannions from down the road in Tullykyne, that I go to the new multi-denominational secondary school seven miles away in Galway, and that I don't have a boyfriend. 'Ah it's all ahead of you now.' She whispers when she's asking questions, and it's hard not to answer her digging. 'I have two sons,' she tells me, 'but they're a bit too old for you yet, love. I don't like their girlfriends much, but still, you're too young.' She sighs whenever she talks about her sons. They're both away at college, that's why she's working in this kip, she says.

I scan through the next customer's groceries: low-fat yoghurt, multi-grain bread, organic milk, *The Times*, a six-pack of beer and a tub of Ben & Jerry's. Cookies and cream, my favourite. I can't stop thinking about food. My mouth is watering, longing for something other than the taste of sugar-substitute and mint. Something tart, really tart, like sloes in late September, picked off the blackthorn trees before the frosts get them. The kind of tart that makes you scrunch up your face, numbs your lips on the way in.

My body mass index is 32 and I have to get it down to 27 before any surgeon will go near me, even with the full amount of cash saved. Six grand, it's going to cost. That's 923 hours in Supervalu.

Maybe it's time to switch to fruit-flavoured chewing gum.

Break-time and I head out with Nora for ten minutes of second-hand smoke. I have a small bottle of diet Seven-Up and a pack of cherry menthol gum to keep me going.

'Normally there are four of us on, but Breeda will be fine on her own for a few minutes,' Nora says, waving at her. 'Back in five minutes,' she calls. 'Ten,' she says under her breath. 'Don't worry, we'll take the full ten. Maybe fifteen.'

This is my first proper summer job. Babysitting doesn't really count.

'Johnny, have you met our new colleague,' she says to the man stacking cases of Barry's Tea in the corner of the stockroom. He shakes his head, but doesn't look up at me. Nora's whispering again. 'Not the full picnic, if you know what I mean, but the only one who has survived working down in stock longer than a year. Doesn't talk much.'

I rest my back against the doorframe, allow myself to drift off to Nora's chatter about everyone who works here. Official Supervalu news source. I try not to think about food. I'm on the chewing gum diet, only allowed one meal a day. My mother hasn't noticed yet.

Johnny is shifting boxes from the loading bay over to the pallet next to me. 'You have lovely green eyes,' he says when he has to get past. 'Like the green on a bottle of Fairy liquid.'

He's standing right in front of me, looking down, all his weight on one foot with the other stretched out, ready to bolt out the door. I'm stuck there, and I can't help looking at him, at the piece of stubble on his cheek that he missed when shaving, at the way he already has lines on his forehead, furrowed between his eyebrows. All I can hear is Nora laughing.

Bib. Bip. Bip. Three Mars bars, a can of Coke, a packet of cheese and onion Taytos. Three euro and thirty-four cents. Two flat-chested skinny girls, their hair artfully tousled with heavy fringes. They're a year older than me, go to a different school. One of them has her boyfriend with her. Danny Collins. We used to hang out together in primary school. He says hi, he's nice enough, but he's the same as all the boys I know. It's as though he's afraid of curves and mounds of girl-flesh. I try to remember what my body looked like before I hit twelve, but all I can remember is the feeling of climbing the railings and racing in Ross Sports. No pictures.

When I picture myself now, on a good day I see those Hindu goddesses we learnt about in religious ed class. On a bad day, a lactating sow: another kind of goddess altogether. Or a pair of breasts with me attached.

The music of the scanners' bips, the fluorescent lights, even the cardboard cut-out of the goddess of suntans have settled into a sort of normal. I am no longer sweating.

'Patricia,' Johnny calls, and I keep shifting bottles of water down the checkout, a small bip with each successful pass. 'Patricia, you're wanted,' he says and I realise he's talking to me. My name badge has my official birth-cert name on it, but nobody ever calls me that. I'm Tricia at home and school, Trish to my friends. Patricia makes me sound as if I could be someone else. I kind of like that idea. Someone whose opinion counts.

'In a minute,' I tell him, and he wanders off to the back office, via the shelves of wine and down past the crisp packets. Johnny never takes the direct route if he can help it.

'Right, Patricia,' Mr O'Connor—Mike—says, and I don't correct him. I like the idea of this new me, stretched out to three syllables, a grown-up me. He wants to sort out the rota, which shifts I'm able to work for the next few weeks. I can't talk much, I'm too nervous for anything other than simple answers.

I tell him the days I'm free (all of them, really) and I think I answer all his questions. The lack of food is starting to kick in. I hope I've been making sense. He comes around to the front of his desk, leans against it so I have to look up at him. His leg is right beside mine, I'm not wearing tights and I can almost feel his trousers against the side of my bare calf. I can feel his heat.

'So, is there anything you need to ask, no? No problems?'

I tell him everything is just fine and then I have to stand up so I can do back to work, except that when I get up out of the chair he doesn't move, so I'm standing right close to him and he's between me and the door. I'm almost the same height as him, and he doesn't move away, doesn't say anything. He watches me.

Fuck. Do I turn and go back around the chair, walk the long way to get to the door, or do I wait for him to move?

Except he's not moving and he's the boss so I can't exactly tell him to shift out of the way, so I turn around, go the long way. Almost trip over the leg of the chair.

'Let me know if you need anything,' he says to me as I open the door. I trust myself to nod, that's it.

My mother makes it to twelve noon before she calls in, my little brother in tow. 'Look what I got you,' she says, confident and urgent. She holds out a small bag to me, pulls apart the handles. It's a bra. 'New minimiser,' she whispers. 'Best on the market, apparently. NASA technology, designed by engineers.'

As if that will change my life.

My little brother is having none of it. 'How come she gets an engineered bra and all I get is Jar Jar Binks?' he asks, perfect elocution and at the top of his voice. I could kill him, but at least he has distracted my mother. She pays for her bottle of Ernest and Julio, giving out to him instead of me.

'Will you try it,' she whispers to me.

I will, I'll wear her space-engineered bra with NASA technology, right up until I can get under the surgeon's knife. However many bips of the scanner it takes.

I only take a half-hour lunch break. It's not like I have much to do—chewing gum doesn't take up much time. I escape to the bookshop for a few minutes, skim the titles and read a few pages of the new Holly Black book. But I'm saving all my money, so it'll have to wait for a trip to the library.

Breeda, the other checkout girl, sends me out the back for Nora. She wants her lunch break but doesn't want to leave me on my own. I kind of feel the same way. Nora isn't in her usual smoking spot and there's no sign of her in the staff toilets either.

Johnny is standing in the middle of the stockroom, staring at a stack of pasta sauces. I say hello, not expecting anything back, slowing down to see if I can spot why he's staring at sauce.

'It's the tomatoes,' he says, as if he knows what I'm thinking. 'The way they go so easily from smooth plump globes to mush. And how different they taste after they do.' He's finished talking and turns around to look at me. Nods. Turns out his eyes are hazel.

And I barely register Nora leaving Mr O'Connor's—Mike's—office, back into the supermarket to finish out her shift, or Mr O'Connor coming to the door of his office a moment or so later. I can't stop looking at Johnny and the crates of pasta sauce behind him. I had never really seen tomatoes before, never really considered them, or their sauce.

'Your eyes really are so green,' he says, seriously, as if they're the only green in the world, and I feel as though my eyes are me and I am my eyes, the only part of my body that exists.

'Johnny,' shouts Mr O'Connor. 'Johnny!'

Snap, and I'm back to regular me, and Johnny is just Johnny the slightly touched stock-boy.

'Get away from those sauces and do what I asked you—the shelves need more milk and vegetables, get them out there now before the women start to give out.' He walks back into the office and pretends to mutter to himself, though I can perfectly hear him. 'Soft fucker, only reason I keep him on is his shoulders and strong back, that and his father. Daft bastard.'

As if he can sense my back rising with these words, he turns around. 'And you, are you going to hang around and go soft with him, or are you going to get back into work like I hired you to do?'

I don't say a word. I look back to see Johnny's head slumped forward, closed off. I walk to the fluorescent-lit doorway, walk the wrong way through the exit-only door, back to my ergonomic chair, and the cardboard suntan goddess still smiling at me.

One hour to clock-off time. Only 916 working hours left to go until I can get back to my real self.

QUICK REACTION FORCE

The day the fish got stuck in the letterbox, that's when she knew she couldn't stop. Margaret looked around her living room, holding the limp mackerel in one hand, out in front of her, as an offering. The photo of Lorraine looked back at her, from its dust-free perch on the mantelpiece. Her daughter centre-stage, as always.

'It's the fish I feel sorry for!' she shouted at the wall her living room shared with the neighbour's front room. They weren't home to hear her.

Light filtered through the gap between the curtains. Margaret worried about the fading, that her good carpet might go from deep swirls of brown to flat beige. Never mind her three-piece suite, the one she had bought after years of saving, the caramel-coloured damask, a luxury a mother could only afford when she had sent her daughter out into the world. Every stain showed on it, every drop of spilled tea. Even Jack knew to sleep on the rug she left out for him, curling up nose to tail so he wouldn't get dog-hair on the couch.

Four-and-a-half months since Margaret had seen Lorraine and

this was how she imagined her: her back rigid, her smile formal, the green army uniform casting her skin a paler shade. A two-dimensional figure, no sound connected, no movement. As if a photo had taken the place of her breathing daughter.

'Only a bit over a month till you're out of that place,' she said to the photo. 'And I suppose you'll be as black as all those darkies, out in the sunshine all the time.'

She caught herself, knowing Lorraine would give out to her for saying that, using those words. Her daughter had been excited when the Army told her she'd be spending six months in Liberia. 'Action, Mum. And a chance to see the world. It's why I joined up.'

As bad as your father, can't wait to get away. Sleep with a gun under your pillow. Leave me here to worry about you. Those were the things she wanted to say to Lorraine. 'And have you got all the knickers I bought for ya? They're a hundred percent cotton.' When Lorraine laughed, she added, 'You'll thank me, in that heat, mark my words you'll thank me.' She could hear the sharp edge to her voice, couldn't stop it.

The trouble started when that knacker she had paid to strim the hedge decided he would give it a number one instead of the usual short back and sides. The neighbours had lost it with her, giving out to her as though she had cut it back too short herself, as though she had done it on purpose.

'All our flipping privacy is gone! What did you do that for?' the pair of them had asked her. She wondered would they speak to her like that if her husband was still around.

The following Saturday, when she had emptied rugs and chairs and vanity units out onto the path leading to her front door so she could get a head start on her spring cleaning, someone had scribbled *mad bitch* onto every piece of wood that would take the purple chalk marks. Then they had written it in clumsy capital letters across the pavement outside her gate.

'What is this place coming to,' she muttered as she wiped the chalk off her furniture. 'And now I'll have to borrow a hose to clean that path.'

That night, she let Jack roam into next-door's garden to have a poo. 'Good boy,' she said as she gave him a dog biscuit. 'My great little lad.'

Margaret hoped one of them would step in it. Her neighbours were a young couple, renting off the council. She hated the cosiness of that word: neighbours. As if there was some bond between them, beyond the coincidence of shared walls.

Most of her old neighbours had moved away, cashing in on the rising property prices and moving out to the suburbs. These young bucks didn't even know that she had once worked for the government, supported her family. Or that she had been fired when she got married, because that was what they did back in the late sixties. She could see the way they looked at her, that they couldn't imagine anything but an ageing woman living on her own. Useless to everyone, one blade of a pair of scissors.

When things got really bad, when they had taken to spitting curses at her every time she walked past, she turned to Hank Williams. He sang 'Cold Cold Heart' at midnight, full blast on Lorraine's CD player. My God but could that man write a song. She snuggled down under the duvet, the electric blanket turned up high. She had slept through years of her husband's overweight snoring, she figured Hank would sing her right to sleep.

'Just like your father!' Margaret said again, this time when Lorraine told her she was asking for an extended tour of duty. Since Liberia's post civil war elections, there was talk of the UN moving back into Sierra Leone. More mopping up after other people's trouble.

Christie had been the same, living for his tours. He had been in love with the Army, with its mysterious rituals. One of the reasons she only had one child, all those trips. Margaret never liked being on her own and she found out early on that there is no loneliness quite like being left with a baby for six months at a time. Sleep, feed, nappy change. Sleep, feed, nappy change. Later she wondered if it was the right thing to do, to have left herself with one daughter to depend on, one daughter who took after the wayward side of the family. Sometimes life seemed easier if you treated it as if it were somebody else's story and you were just borrowing it for a while.

'Did it annoy you to die of a heart attack?' she asked Christie's memorial card. 'All them fries. Death by chips and sausages. Not something you could get a medal for.'

When she thought about it, she was the one who killed him, all that cooking in lard and butter. Maybe she should feel guilty about it.

After the fish came through the door, she started putting things through her next-door neighbour's letterbox: newspaper clippings of the new pope, an empty box of Milk Tray. Once she put in a rusty knife that she couldn't figure out how to get rid of. Late at night, while they were all safely curled up in front of the TV, she would take Jack out for his walk and sneak right up their path. She didn't think of it as revenge, exactly. More like standing up for herself.

As long as that couple did not open the door on her, she did not care who saw her. Some nights, when she was feeling bold, she would wave at the young lads who congregated down the road. They were too young to scare her, barely teenagers, just a handful of the local boys who wanted to stay out late and had yet to figure out how to talk to girls.

One of them broke away from the group, sauntered over to her. 'Got a fag, granny?'

Margaret knew she should be offended, but she just shook her head. Sometimes when she saw boys his age, part of her would think: aah he's lovely, don't I wish I had a son to look after me. As if she didn't have enough trouble with one daughter.

While she waited for the PC to boot up, she sat down next to it, on the edge of her daughter's bed and read over what she had written on the lined paper, her handwriting meticulous.

Dear Lorraine,

It is very cold here today, and wet as usual. My joints are feeling it, but the doctor says that is normal enough for someone my age. I could have killed him for saying it, but he is such a nice young man and remember how I didn't even want to stay with him when he took over Dr Winter's practice. Liz was asking for you, I told her you would be home for your birthday, that your tour would be up by then. Would you like the usual dinner, or should I just go for a big roast beef? Let me know, I'll make something you would like. I'm trying to keep this short like you asked me to so I will say goodbye for now and don't forget to keep your head covered in that heat.

Love Mum.

Lorraine always gave out to her when her emails were too long—she claimed the terminal was only part of their welfare time, not her own personal communications centre. They were her exact words, 'personal communications centre'. Margaret wondered where she picked up this lingo.

She propped up the sheet of paper next to the computer, and her eyes moved between the screen, the paper and the keyboard as she typed up the email, using both index fingers to punch the keys. Even Lorraine considered this an advance. When her daughter had taught Margaret how to send an email, she could only type with the index finger of her right hand.

As she clicked *send*, the last time she talked to Lorraine came back to her, how her daughter's voice sounded older over the phone. As if she had grown since her boots touched Liberian soil. How all she had to give her daughter was the news that her test results were clear, that everything else was exactly how she left it, how for the next forty-three days Margaret would try to keep it that way.

She waited eight days for retaliation. Eight days of pushing things through that couple's door, and at least half of those times leaving a gift from Jack on their doorstep. Her nerves were starting to get the better of her when a Guard rang her doorbell.

'Are you Margaret Helen Moore?'

She nodded, too frightened to speak. My baby, my Lorraine, oh my God Lorraine.

'I have here a summons for you to appear in court, Mrs Moore.'

'What?' Her shock made her speak louder than she intended. She practically shouted, 'You what?'

'A summons. You've been asked to appear in court on charges of breaching the peace.' The Guard handed the papers over to her, nodding as he did.

Margaret tried to take it in, tried to control herself in front of him. Then she burst out laughing.

'Right so,' he said, backing away from the door, not sure how to react. He was young, too young to be in uniform. Too young for her to feel bad about her reaction. She closed the door, walked back into the sitting room, summons in hand. 'You useless shower,' she shouted at the wall, hoping they were home to hear her.

That night, she treated them to Patsy Cline at full volume. She ignored the thumping on the wall of her bedroom. Stayed awake, though.

When she did sleep, she slept late, dreaming about armies of boys and life-size fish. Groggy with the late hour, she ran off to her meeting in the community centre. Sometimes she thought it would be good to have a paying job again, maybe a career. Just so she would have money that went beyond the ESB bill and her roots touched up once a month. Even the few euro Lorraine sent her every month meant she could go for tea in O'Connor's as a treat.

'Well, the test results came back clear—'

'I know Mum, you already told me,' Lorraine said, the line

crackling, as if it could barely contain the breadth of her voice.

'Oh, right … Well, just to let you know that everything's going ahead for Liz's wedding anyway. You'll be back for that, won't you?'

Big sigh. Lorraine did not even bother trying to hide her impatience. 'I dunno, I should be, I guess.'

Margaret took her turn, told her a bit of local gossip, as she always did. She thought it was important to keep her daughter up on the local goings-on, so Lorraine would not feel too homesick while she was away and to make it easier for her to re-adjust when she got back. It was all she could do to stop herself from telling her daughter to talk properly.

'And of course, the little bitch is at it again, throwing the rubbish from the street into my front garden,' Margaret said.

'What? What are you on about?'

Margaret couldn't tell if it was shock or annoyance that made Lorraine's reply so abrupt. This impatience had developed over some years—she figured her daughter must have perfected it as a teenager. She could still remember the day she brought Lorraine out to help her with the Christmas shopping, how she laughed at her when Margaret kept asking the shop assistants what country things were from. 'Oh Mum,' she had said, 'like it makes any difference whether a lamp was made in China or Germany. It's not like you won't buy it anyway.' It took Lorraine a full thirty-eight minutes in the shopping centre to find a schoolmate she could skip off with, even less time to make Margaret feel like some strange creature, a 'mother' who should be handled a particular way, with thick hide gloves and sarcasm.

'You know, love, that little bitch next door, and all her carrying on. I told you about it the last time you were on the phone to me.'

'What carrying on?'

'I'm sure I told you already, you know, about the writing on the path outside the house—'

'No you didn't—'

'The fish in the letterbox? I'm sure I told you—'

'No, Mum, you never told me. Trust me, I would have remembered that.'

A silence weighed between them. Margaret knew she would be the one to break it.

'Oh well, it's just a bit of nonsense, really—honestly, I'm trying not to let it get to me,' she said, wondering if the lie sounded as bad on the other end of the phone line.

Jack wasn't waiting for her when she got home. He usually sat up on the front windowsill, a little terrier statue looking out at the world going by. When she would lift the latch on the gate, he would come running down to greet her, his stumpy tail spinning.

This evening, there was no sign of him, even when she turned the key in the lock, calling his name. 'Jack, ya little rascal, where are ya?' she called. 'C'mere Jack, I have a treat for ya. Ja-ack!'

Margaret flicked the latch on the door so the draught could not close it. She cleaned out the ashes and lit the fire, not wanting to waste the oil.

'Ja-ack,' she called out any time she passed the open door.

After tea, she took the latch off and slammed the door. 'He can scratch if he wants to get in. Feckin' dog. As bad as that daughter of mine, putting me to this much worry.'

She dusted the living room and mopped the kitchen floor twice. Margaret perched on the edge of her golden sofa and kept one ear on the nine o'clock news, the other listening out for the door. More stories from abroad: nothing about Liberia or Sierra Leone. She waited past the weather to see who would be on the Late Late Show. Politicians and Big Brother celebrities. Not her thing, really.

As she lifted her coat off the peg in the hallway, a voice made her turn around.

'And would you ever pick up some of those little sausages while you're out—y'know, the ones the butcher does. And one of those cream buns, ah come on, just one won't harm me.'

Margaret turned around, her coat hanging off her shoulder, mid-gesture.

It was Christie again, standing with his arm high up on the doorjamb, leaning his weight onto one foot so his belly stuck out. She wanted to reach out, touch him gently or maybe give him a slap, make up for all the years she missed out, but she knew he would be gone as soon as she moved across the gap. So she stood as still as she could, her sleeve halfway up, afraid to breathe in case he faded back into the air he came from. Knowing it would happen anyway.

What she would have given to have a massive row with him. To fill up the hall, the kitchen, the front room with the ringing of their raised voices one more time.

When the phone rang, Margaret had a feeling it would be Lorraine. But it turned out to be Nancy, one of the other army mothers.

'I just wanted to let you know I was talking to Julie today and Lorraine is much better.'

'What?'

'She said Lorraine's much better. I thought you might be worried, so I just wanted to let you know, in case you didn't get to talk to her this week.'

'Oh, thanks,' Margaret said and hung up without saying goodbye. She wanted Nancy off the phone in case Lorraine was trying to get through.

Margaret had visions of Lorraine driving over a landmine, or on patrol in some village when rebels attacked, or catching some rare African illness, or getting assaulted by one of those foreigners at the camp. On and on her mind flew, each scenario played out to the worst. Margaret tried to get through to the barracks in Athlone, to find out what had happened. No one could tell her anything, so they put her onto Headquarters and she knew before she even talked to them that they wouldn't tell her anything.

She pictured exploding limbs and deliriums and comas and bloody bullet holes in her only daughter. 'Give me the number of whoever's in charge over in Liberia,' she said to the man in Dublin.

Then strange single rings.

'Yes, you've reached Camp Clara.'

'In Liberia?' Margaret asked, not waiting for a yes before she launched into a scrambled plea to put Lorraine on the line. And no, she didn't mind holding.

'Hello, Mum?'

'Jesus, Lorraine, you can talk.'

'Hunh?'

'I was so worried. And the rest of you—are you very bad? Was it rebels?'

'No!'

'Not them foreigners, I'll—'

'Mum, no, nobody, it was nobody but myself.' Lorraine told her how she'd been on long-range patrol and had stumbled over a small hole—a dirt pothole really—and pulled her shoulder. 'A small tear in my rotator cuff, apparently. I'll be on camp duty till Wednesday week.'

'Oh,' said Margaret.

'So I'm fine.'

'Oh.'

Neither of them said anything for a moment.

'Well I'll go so. If you're sure you're okay.'

'Sure.'

Margaret hung up the phone, walked from the living room to the kitchen and back again, wondered why Jack wasn't home yet.

The air outside was bitter cold, her breath freezing the moment it left her mouth, making her look as if she was smoking. Margaret walked as far as her gate, calling Jack.

The boys stood at the end of the road, watching her. As she

headed towards them, they shifted their stances, shoving hands into pockets and lighting cigarettes they didn't even want. Anything to keep themselves in constant motion. She would bet their mothers wished all that energy went into keeping their rooms clean.

'Have you seen my little Jack?' she called over to them, not waiting until she reached the corner.

They all looked down the other side of the road, said nothing.

'Little terrier, y'know, a Jack Russell. He's gone missing.'

The one who had called her a granny shrugged his shoulders. 'I dunno.'

Something about the way he would not look at her made her suspicious. 'What have you done to my little Jack?'

'Ask your neighbours, you crazy bat,' he said, finally looking straight at her.

Margaret looked around at them all. The rest of them would not let their eyes meet hers. A sharp gust of wind blew up, took her breath.

She marched back up the road, her back straight, her arms stiff with what they might do.

Brickies had abandoned a partly built wall. Barely slowing down, she bent down and grasped a brick in her right hand, swinging it as she stomped past her own gate.

They had left the curtains open. Margaret stepped out onto their patch of dying grass and watched them for a moment. Himself sat in a leather armchair, laughing at whatever Pat Kenny's guest was saying on the *Late Late*. Herself had stretched out on the couch, her head propped up on a cushion so she could see the TV. Margaret wanted to shout at them, rouse them from their cosy shell, then laugh in their faces. She wanted them to see her when they looked out, actually see her.

Tears burnt the corners of her eyes, her throat aching with the effort of holding back. Every ounce of anger she possessed filtered to her right hand until it pulsed, shaking the brick she still held. She lifted her arm behind her, the brick pulling her weight back until it felt like the most natural thing to do—to bring her arm over, let the brick fly through the air.

A shapeless load lifted as she watched that red brick arc towards the sitting room window. She smiled when she heard the crash of the plate glass, her expression distorting as she shouted, 'You BASTARDS!'

Margaret turned and ran out through the gate, forgetting her age, her coat flapping in the wind as she ran up past the boys guarding their corner. She didn't stumble until she reached the new road, and the lights of the cars forced her to close her eyes, all the time calling 'Jack! Ja-ack!'

IT'S HAPPENING AGAIN

The two boys are kicking a ball, back and forth, back and forth and she is sitting down on the bench, watching them. Well, keeping an eye on them really, to make sure they don't get too close to the new houses that edge the green. She remembers when this was all farmland, cows grazing, brown ones mostly, not picture-postcard white and black ones.

Rebecca's mother and the mother of that little shaved-head fella from Finn's class come round the bend, head her way. Get ready, chit-chat, remember the required words.

They walk right past. And like that, she's gone.

It's a funny feeling, invisibility, and she wonders if she has become more solid, the same shade or shape as the bench. Or if she's transparent, something you could pass through and only dimly register a sense of unease.

The boys haven't noticed yet. But then, they're used to not seeing her. To them, she's as background as cows on grass. She watches as Finn kicks the ball hard, watches it veer past Colm's head, land bash splat against Rebecca's mother's right shoulder. Rebecca's mother raises her voice—angry syllables drift back over to the bench—gives her mind's worth to the boys. They rescue the ball, pay no attention. Maybe she's disappearing too.

The clouds speed up overhead, the wind picking up, and she thinks she can see cow patties scattered over the grass. A group of little girls, six-years-old at the most, straggle over to her bench, set themselves up on it: she's not even there. They argue about whether or not their mothers can see them over here, whether it's safe to practice the super-secret code.

'It's the only way to make sure we're the only ones in the club,' the curly-haired girl says. They all nod solemnly. Secrecy is important. And invisibility. The ability to exist outside the awareness of the people who care about you.

She tests her voice. 'Whatever you do, don't get caught,' she tells them, but they don't hear her.

A football tumbles under the bench and she lifts her foot out of the way. 'Hey Mum, have you got something to eat, we're starvin' marvin here,' her eldest says, jogging over towards her.

And she's back. The coven of girls heads down the slope to the safety of their mothers, and she is responsible, again.

GHOSTGIRL

I can still see myself, back then. My secret power was that I could become invisible. Mum taught me how. She didn't mean to. But after *Nicola get out of the fuckin' way* and *Nicola will you ever let your father into the loo so he can do his business* had sunk into my toddler brain and pissing on the floor hadn't helped, I copped it—just disappear, so she can't see you.

On her first day back on the drink when I was four-and-a-half, I learnt the other trick: don't ask questions. When she came roaring into the living room one of the nights my father left, I tried it out: before the first letter of my name came out of her mouth, I settled on the floor at the end of the couch where Jimmy always sat, tucked my knees up under my chin and watched the bits of dust float past me, like little stars in the sunshine. I wanted to be one of them, a little star, and I curled up tight, taught myself to breathe slowly and quietly, listened to Mum's far away voice lash Jimmy and Paul. Waited there till my father came home from one of his jobs around Sligo, and then Mum might fire something under the grill for tea.

At national school, I was always careful about when I made myself invisible. The teachers were suspicious of me. One of them told me I was too cute, but she was ancient and it wasn't long before she left. I tried not to disappear in class. On the playground Gemma McGarry would get the other fourth class girls to whisper 'slut' whenever I walked past. I had to disappear next to the concrete wall every break-time. There wasn't much I could do about it inside school. Eventually, 'slut' turned into 'crusty slut' and Gemma and her crowd of girls would skirt an arm's length around me. I didn't dream that when we went to the Mercy, me and Gemma would be best friends by the end of First Year. Maybe she wanted to be a slut too.

*

It was handy to go invisible on the families.

I have been through five families. The first one only lasted three weeks, but that wasn't their fault. Mum managed to convince my social worker that she could manage just fine, now that she was on her own again. She wouldn't tell anyone why her latest man had kicked her back out to the other side of the estate. The second family took me in for the summer I turned eight, when Mum went back to your man for more. He only let her stay the summer with him, then turfed her out after she lost her job at the bread factory. I went back to the house with her, but I didn't say a word. The third and fourth families were for the odd week here and there, they hardly counted. Mum always called them my 'holidays'. Family number five though, they were a new thing to me.

First off, when I walked in the front door, Mrs Shaughnessy reached out, both arms open. As if she wanted to give me a hug. I was twelve years old, way past hugging people I didn't know. My social worker sort of shook her head, and Mrs Shock let her arms drop, sort of like a deflated balloon. My heart sank. I could just tell it was going to be hard to disappear on this one. See, they have to want you to not be there so you can make yourself invisible. This one was going to be tricky. She wasn't just a watcher, she was a wanter.

Mrs Shock led me into the front room, the room without a telly, and told me to make myself at home. 'Yes, Mrs Shock,' I said. She told me to call her Geraldine. 'Yes Mrs Shock,' I said. I'd heard of women like her from some of the other girls, but I'd never met one before. One of the ones that wasn't taking me in for the money. The more she wanted to get into whatever I was doing, the more I went the other way.

That was when trouble started. I got the curse, it leaked through my skirt in the middle of class. Found I couldn't make myself invisible anymore: I had to fuck off out of the house if I didn't want to be noticed. Three missed tea-times in a row and she'd report me to the social worker. I'd be on warning after warning, out with Gemma and the girls, sculling back any drink we could get our hands on, trying our best to get away from them all, having some fun, a spliff, some tabs down by the Garavogue River when one of the lads had enough.

Mrs Shock drove me mad with her soft eyes and her *but why's*. Always trying to get me to talk, then talking at me when I wouldn't bother saying a word. By my fifth out-of-hours review, the social worker copped where this was headed, let Mrs Shock off the hook, moved me on to the next family.

*

The current family is one I'd heard of from another girl like me. The hostel house. That's what it is, a hostel you sleep in and get your fish fingers and chips in. Anne O'Leary runs it on her own, fits her five scaldy children around it, and never mentions her husband or how he went off with the hairdresser. Sligo is small enough that we all know the story.

I do everything I can to stay out of the place, hang out in the McGarry's house whenever I can, just up from my old house in Garavogue Villas. Gemma and Linda are sitting on the sofa beside me, watching *You're A Star*. Anthony, their dad, is in the armchair reading the *Sunday Mirror*.

How long do you have to stare at someone before they'll turn around? With Anthony, it only takes a few seconds. But he's a suspicious bastard, always waiting for the next wrong move. He trained in the army. He didn't stay long, but he was stationed over in Kildare and no one ever found out what happened. Ray Gorman reckons he killed another soldier. (That's the word around town, anyway.)

'What're you gawping at?'

'Nothing,' I say. Nobody can find out about us or he'll flip.

'You set for tomorrow?' Linda asks. I'm supposed to see the social worker about my school attendance record.

'Yeah, it'll be the usual crap,' I say, and keep quiet about how I really feel. My tummy is at me and I feel like crying whenever I think about being lectured at by that woman. Or worse still, the quiet gaps where she doesn't say a word. But three social workers down the line, I know that the best thing to do is shut up and let them see what they want to see, fill in the blank parts of you to suit their own ideas.

*

'Trouble will find you,' Mum said the last time she let me stay with her. She had that edge on her, the one she gets when she's mixing other stuff with the drink. I kept my mouth shut, hunted around for the remote control. I kept my hands busy.

'You've always been one that attracted bad stuff,' she said. 'Just like your father. Useless git.'

I didn't say anything, I didn't tell her I'm nothing like my useless father and nothing like my useless mother. Even though I could've shouted it in her face. I shrugged, and that was enough to wind her up.

'Mark my words, missy, you'll fuck up big-time and you'll be lucky if you live to regret it. You think you're so clever. Hah. Wait'll you see the kind of crap life has waiting for you.'

That's when I put the hole in the door. In fairness, it was a cheap hollow wood door, but when I let a kick fly at it, I was shocked that my foot went all the way through.

Mum's face froze, and the rest of her did too. She looked so funny standing there that I almost laughed.

'I'm out of here,' I said. She didn't stop me, she didn't care enough.

*

It's the day after my fourteenth birthday. I've got the pink phone Anthony gave me stuffed into the back pocket of my jeans. I don't care that he didn't have the box for it. The outline of it feels good against my left cheek, reminds me of yesterday afternoon. I couldn't stay out past six, the family I'm with had an appointment with my social worker, and I'm already on a last warning. I'm old enough now to know when to show up and keep my mouth shut. Too bad Mum won't do the same.

She still won't take me back, says I'm too much trouble. I just want my freedom.

My room this time is on the back of the house. Sun shines right into it first thing in the morning, wakes me up and wrecks my head. Same crap peach curtains as my last room. This is the room I go to when I'm not in school, or when I'm not over at McGarry's, or when I need to sleep. Magnolia walls and the window left open to stop the mould and a new bed every September. I'm the first one to sleep on this one so far. Lucky me.

Tonight we get to celebrate before he heads off for the weekend. I told Mrs House (that's what I call her behind her back) I'd be over at Gemma's, and I will. But the McGarry girls—Gemma and her sister and her mum—are heading up to Enniskillen to do some shopping for Christmas and Jamie's off at a mate's house, so me and Anthony will have the place to ourselves. We'll watch a DVD maybe, have some fun. He's the first man I've ever been in love with.

It feels different with Anthony. Not like the flat kisses of boys, where I know they're trying to figure out how far they can push it. With Anthony, it's more like that tingling feeling you get when one of your mates brushes your hair or runs the straightener through it.

Me and Gemma used to talk about what we'd like to be when we grew up. We would do up each other's hair, put loads of coloured hairclips in and have bits of it up. I always said I'd have a pink salon in town, my very own place with pink chairs and a pink sign out the front and everything else in black. That was when we were little, though. I still think I might try and get into hairdressing, if I can stick school long enough to get onto a Fás course.

Sometimes when everyone leaves me alone and the house is empty and quiet, I sit up on the bed and pull the quilt up around me and I daydream about what I could do if I wasn't here, didn't have to put up with other people's houses and social workers and bitch mothers. If I could just feel like I feel when I'm with Anthony, all the time. Melt into him.

Anthony started noticing me when I turned into a woman. I'd always hung out in their house, back as long as I could remember. When I'd started calling down to the girls, I'd only lived five doors down. I knew things had changed when he called me by my real name, and not just *love*, like he called all his girls. I caught him watching me a few times, back when I turned thirteen and I finally fit into a proper bra.

The first time Anthony got me on my own, he just kissed me. Later, when Gemma and Linda and Jamie fell back into the house with whipped cones from the ice-cream van, he whispered, 'Don't tell anyone. Our secret.'

I still haven't had my time of the month. And even though I'm wrecked tired, sleeping is hard. When I finally drop off, I keep having the same dream: I'm swimming through the air, my legs have turned into a tail with fins and I'm going as fast as I can. Sometimes it's Mum, sometimes it's my father, but tonight Anthony is next to me. When I wake up, I'm reaching out, as if I'm grabbing onto him, or pushing him away.

A stone taps the window of the bedroom. I have my own room since that last girl beat me up over a broken CD player. It's Gemma, I don't have to look out. She can't stand Mrs House or the brats, so she always just fires a stone up at the window to let me know she's here. I lean out the window to see what she wants. I only saw her in school an hour ago.

'C'mon up to the Four Lights,' she says.

Sounds better than sitting in this place. I sneak downstairs. Mrs House has left her handbag on the last step; she must be going out again. I find a fiver in her wallet and head out for chips with Gemma.

She's full of bounce as we walk along the path past the old jail and she tells me about a girl from our class, up the duff by a fuckin' buff. We both laugh hard at that one, but on the inside I imagine telling Gemma that she's going to be an auntie.

'Got a smoke?' she asks, but I don't, I've been cutting down on them 'cause Anthony says he doesn't like the taste of John Player Blue on a girl.

The girls are waiting for us outside the chipper and I have to be careful to keep my secret. I'm all excited with a little Anthony growing inside of me and this means I'll be able to get my own house and no more of other people's families and I'll have my own money and I almost tell Gemma and the girls but then I think of what Anthony would do if I told them first. So I breathe it all in, invisible, until Anthony gets back from Manchester. Wait. Deep breaths, try not to remember the last afternoon I melted into Anthony, lost myself and didn't have to be me, free of the hassle and no family and six different houses in my fourteen years, and nothing that would let me say MINE. Better than vodka, even.

I text him, even though Anthony had said never to ring him or text him again.

Miss u loads Mega news 4 u :-D Nx

I panic a bit as I hit send. Anthony can be funny about things.

The night he gave me the phone I'd sent him a message. Just a howya text. He had almost lost it with me then, I heard it in his voice when he rang me back. 'Don't you ever do that again,' he said. 'I gave you that phone so *I* could ring *you*, got it. There's some credit on it, ring your friends if you want to. But I don't want to hear from you.' His voice sounded very calm, but I could hear his breathing, fast and harsh.

'Right,' I said, hoping I sounded cool. I didn't want him to be pissed off at me. 'I was just trying it out.'

He had hung up without saying goodbye.

MEET M @ D OLD ABBY @ 9. T x

It's Tuesday, and I'd already had a row with Mrs House over some dirty dishes. She starts at me when she catches me in the hallway with my jacket on, did I do my homework and don't I know it's a school night and I'm on probation already and I shouldn't be going out, and on and on. 'I'll ring the social worker,' she says, as if that'll make me stay.

I walk fast past St Anne's and cut through the car park. My hand keeps sneaking up to my belly. I'm excited to see Anthony again and now I'll finally get to tell him about little Anthony, about my baby and I'm set now.

My heart is flying it, I can feel it thumping against my ribs, and I slow down a bit, check my hair is still smooth, look down at my skirt and skinny top. I have my push up bra on and my breasts look massive now. It took me ages to figure out what to wear, I wanted to look cool and pretty and sexy. I want to look the way I feel. I want to look as though my life is just starting new.

The sky is just getting proper dark and the outline of the abbey ruins is black against the low clouds. It doesn't feel like rain, though.

I didn't bring my jacket.

At one end the black railings only poke a short way over the stone wall. Someone has tipped over a wheelie bin, and I step onto it, grasp the metal, pull myself up onto the wall. From up here I can see the whole of the abbey, all the way down into the inside. I think I can see Anthony's outline over by the far wall.

The streetlights cast long shadows across the old stone and cut grass. I can hear the sounds of a sitcom from someone's open window. The cold slips past me.

Everyone else in Abbeyquarter is sitting inside in front of the telly. Sligo is mine. From up here, I can see the entire town, how it will be, my whole life spread out in front of me, and for the first time since I can remember I don't want to disappear, I don't want to have to avoid getting caught anymore.

The invisible world doesn't matter anymore. My hand holds the low part of my belly and I'm floating up over the black metal railings, swimming through the night air to the grass on the other side.

I walk over to Anthony. He's leaning against the wall of the old stone abbey, his arms crossed, waiting for me.

'Well,' he says. All edges.

The hurley leaning against the wall beside him is invisible, and the flex of muscle under his skin is invisible and the edge of his brain that has turned is invisible.

I don't see any of it; I have a new baby inside of me and my life ahead of me.

SEIZURES

Eileen is listening, something that requires more effort these days. She hears Gabriel shoo Frasier out of the freshly turned soil, and peeks through the living room window: Gabriel is out the front, hard at work with the garden claw. Frasier wants to help though, thinks digging up the earth is a great game to play. His limp is getting worse, she notices, as he backs away from Gabriel with a carefulness that a boundy dog shouldn't show.

She used to think she'd like gardening—plump ripe tomatoes, sweet carrots, peas eaten straight from the pod. When the boys were growing up she persuaded Gabriel to put in some raised beds for vegetables. She spent one season battling with weeds and said never again. Out here in the peat hills of Moycullen she has enough of the natural side of life; unlike Gabriel, she doesn't feel the need to add to it.

It starts to rain and Eileen hurries outside, pulls the clothes off the line, even though it's just a shower: dark clouds over one side of the house, pale blue sky on the other. She has a tumble dryer, the one she insisted on buying when they moved into the house, but she only uses it when the rain won't stop; she likes the look of clean bedding strung across the garden, waving with every puff of wind, company somehow. Plus she likes the fresh smell of clothes straight off the line, the comforting bundle of it.

Eileen can't figure out if Gabriel realises she's avoiding him, too. When he starts to react to her shift in mood, she knows Gabriel is liable to lose it with her if she asks the most simple questions: what he wants for dinner, has he seen yesterday's paper.

She thinks of the time she and Gabriel broke up, how she wandered the house while the boys were away at college, a dull thud in her chest that waited for perfect silence to be heard, though she felt it well enough the rest of the time. Eileen remembers the moment it stopped—at Gabriel's rented bedsit, the sight of his shirt hanging above a two-bar heater. That was the moment she took him back, though she didn't actually tell him for a few weeks.

Memories hover along the edges of her mind, brewing carefully, fermenting into something she could almost drink. And the feeling is the same as when her sons were toddlers, all that sleep deprivation, the way colours start to waver, and ordinary objects refuse to stay put. How this seemed normal for a few years, until sleep sneaked back when the boys were settled in school. She grasps these through a fog of forty-odd years: the soft joy of the back of Philip's head, her first-born, the perfect curve of his skull; Matt, bare-bummed on her knee, trying to wriggle away so she wouldn't be able to put a nappy on him; scrums in the back garden on summer evenings, the way the two of them would ignore her calls. And back further, to her early times with Gabriel. Musky fumbles and crossbars home. Eileen calls back these memories to remind her of herself; invisible proof that, yes, she was once this person, in fact, all of them.

Frasier lurches out to the back, with one of Gabriel's secateurs in his mouth, and heads straight to his corner of the garden to add it to his collection of gardening tools and kitchen utensils.

Come back here you mongrel blows around the corner of the house. She watches from behind the clothesline as Frasier pick his way back out front to Gabriel, howling back as if he can talk, his mouth puckered and small with the effort.

The sheets tangle up with the end of her shirt, lifting it so the damp air touches her exposed skin. Reminds her of when she used to wear a bathing suit, sleeveless tops, knee-length skirts without tights. She pauses before she ducks in the back door with the clothes, scans the sky for the strands of refracted light that should be there.

'Ei-leen!'

She runs out of the kitchen, down to the end of the hallway. Gabriel is holding the phone out to her, his face stern, his knuckles showing white. Trouble.

'Hallo,' she says, her eyes on Gabriel as he watches her for a moment, then stomps upstairs when she finds out who it is. 'Oh hello, Sean.'

Turns out to be the vet, asking her to come into the surgery for the test results. He says he needs to see her in person and now her breath catches each time it reaches her sternum.

'Tomorrow,' she hears herself saying. 'After lunch is fine.'

Frasier's howls and the sound of the pot of spuds on the cooker boiling over force her to put down the phone, walk back up to the kitchen, lift the saucepan off the ring, rescue the bag of gammon from Frasier's mouth without starting a game of tug-of-war, sit down on the edge of a chair and start to use her lungs again.

She has fallen through again.

She knows she is in her bedroom and it's nighttime. She can smell Gabriel: a mix of fusty sweat and mint. The eiderdown quilt weighs down on top of her, even though the bed has disappeared from underneath her. In the dark, she can see the outlines of her dresser and bedside table, their edges glowing. This doesn't give her comfort—her eyes are closed, and she would rather not see anything at all.

Eileen feels herself plummeting—the sensation spreads from her chest, rushes all the way to her head, how she felt the time the boys brought her onto the salt and peppershaker at the travelling funfair.

A stranger wearing an electric blue cowboy hat appears in front of her, his eyes hidden by the rim of the hat. She watches as he swivels to check himself out in her bedroom mirror. When he turns into Gabriel, she feels him slipping away. *Thrum thrum*, matching her pulse.

The same mirror, the one she looks in every morning to apply her makeup, smashes into a thousand fragments, and she raises her arm across her head, tries to avoid the jagged chunks and shards small enough to lodge in an eye, or a heart careless enough to get close.

And the falling swells: she is getting bigger and falling faster.

She can just about make out the helpless drilling cry of a newborn baby—oolah oolah oolah over and over—and she knows when the sounds start that this is nearly over: the cry fades slowly into the yelps of Frasier, the smell of dog breath registers somewhere in her mess of a brain, and soon she will be able to move.

Eileen spends the rest of the morning in bed. Seizures have a way of sapping her energy, so when she comes out of one all she wants to do is lie in bed, stare into space. Her *rememory time*, she calls it; she calls back all her loose parts, the bits of her that fly from the side of her brain that stores who she is, the same aspect of her brain that flares with electricity whenever she sends herself mixed signals. She used to think it was God.

Now she feels as if she's wasting it, this other part of her brain. She could be someone else entirely if she wanted. She could be Eileen of the Latin Dance, Eileen of the Road Trip Down a Winding Road. Or even Eileen of the Quiet Time Alone.

She closes her eyes, stretches out flat on her back. Honour first thoughts, she thinks. Honour what little you've learned and your spirit.

'Degenerative myelopathy,' the vet had said when Eileen brought Frasier in to him, a week after she had first noticed Frasier's limp, the way he favoured his hind legs. 'Probably been going on for a while, from the looks of it.'

She's back in to see him again. The tablets that the vet gave her, the ones she has diligently crushed up and mixed in with a spoonful of tinned Pedigree Chum, aren't working anymore. She has tried fish oil supplements, dog vitamins, physiotherapy. But Frasier's bum refuses to stay up, his hip joints slip to the floor and the small yelp he lets out when he tries to get up to chase wood pigeons off Gabriel's seed beds is how she knows the pain is getting worse.

Frasier still looks after her. Still hobbles to her side, barks and nuzzles her hand to tell her the electricity is flying through her brain again. He seems to know when a seizure is on the way long before she notices any of the signs.

To her, the vet is like any other doctor—he shuffles papers, moves his glasses up and down the length of his nose (depending on whether or not he needs to read), doesn't look at her when he gives her the news. 'Frasier is too ill to keep alive. The hind legs will only get worse, then the disease will rapidly spread to the front. There's nothing we can do.' He tells her the medication isn't helping (as if she hasn't noticed this herself). And that she will have to decide soon; Frasier is suffering too much. It's up to her, if—or when—it happens, but he'll get back to her by the end of the week about it, if he hasn't already heard from her.

He uses the word *it* a lot, as if not saying the real word out loud will make the idea of killing her own dog easier. Why does she always have to do this stuff on her own? Why won't Gabriel just do what needs to be done, sit down beside her, offer it up to God (as she used to say). The vet takes his glasses off, starts moving folders into a drawer. Time's up.

Eileen looks over her shoulder before closing the door behind her; all she can see is a man in white, pristine, untouchable.

In the shower, sitting on her old lady seat as Gabriel calls it, Eileen takes her thinking time. Here, naked, she actually likes her body: aches and pains eased by the steam, water running down cleanly along her bumps and slopes. Her body feels useful, satisfactory—it has brought her this far, done whatever has needed to be done. So what if it creaks and groans now. So what if she can't bend down to pick up Frasier's dish.

Behind the blue striped curtain, Eileen considers the euphemisms she could use for Frasier, if he died: Pushing up the daisies. Passed away. Deceased. Demised. Bought a one-way ticket. Popped his clogs. Expired. Departed. Danced the last dance. Sprouted wings. No longer with us. Gone to meet his maker. Stiff. In repose. Resting in peace. Kicked the bucket. Shuffled off the mortal coil. In a better place. Six feet under. Bought the farm. Gone. Late. Checked out.

And worse: Put down. Put to sleep. Done for. Erased. Liquidated. Offed. Executed. Wacked. Terminated. Destroyed. Rubbed out. Bumped off. Finished.

Put out of his misery. Sleeping the big sleep. Worm food. Gone into the fertilizer business. Gone south. Gone to a better place. Given up the ghost. Gone to the big dog in the sky. Gone to be with God.

Frasier looks at her with his deep dog brown eyes, sits down and settles his hind legs as carefully as he can. He's a German Shepherd Labrador cross, not a purebred, so he shouldn't have problems with his hips, but he does anyway. As contrary as everyone else in this house. She has noticed that his hind legs are getting worse, so fast that she can see a change in him from day by day.

Eileen walks slowly on her way down to the kitchen, partly because her own joints are winter stiff, partly so that Frasier can keep up. He takes the stairs the same way her boys did when they first learned to walk: slowly, one limb down at a time.

She can't imagine life without him; ever since Gabriel brought him home seven years ago, thinking a dog might bring her back down to earth, he has been under her feet. But she felt the same way about her two boys, before they headed out into the wide world. Now she wonders how she coped with all that washing and quick cooking and shopping for appetites that reached well beyond the rooftops.

Poor Gabriel, she thinks. Reckoning a dog could control my auras.

The mirror has attracted more dust than the television, and she tries to remember the last time she dusted either of them. A few minutes of wandering around looking at the surfaces in her house, examining the layers of shed skin and dander and fluff on every planar surface and she thinks maybe she should just get out the duster. In the end, it's the mirror she cleans, carefully swiping out the grime that has accumulated in the gilt curves of the frame, going back to the kitchen to get a bottle of vinegar. A splash of balsamic vinegar (she saw one of the chefs in a cookery show use it, but she hasn't used it with food yet) into a bowl of water and she attacks the glass itself, ignoring the blurred reflection of herself, absorbed by gilt, impermeable glass, silver. Gabriel bought this mirror for her when they were first married and had no money. He spotted it in the window of a bric-a-brac shop, when he stopped to look at a transistor radio, and got them to put the mirror away for him. That was back when shops would do that for you, hold onto an item so you could pay off a bit each week until the whole lot was paid for. Back before credit cards and pre-approved loans, back when you had to wait for what you wanted.

The tarnished silver hides the wrinkles, makes her look like an oil painting, one of those old ones that flattered the women in them. No hard edges or hard expressions. Her Snow White mirror.

She supposes it's probably an antique by now. But way back when Gabriel bought it for her it was just old junk, the kind you didn't throw away because it could still be used. That was what everyone did back then—used things, took care of them so they'd last. Even Gabriel learned how to fix a stuck zipper, or darn the heel of a sock. That was back when people didn't worry about highlights or wearing the same skirt two days in a row, there was too much TB, and if the lungs didn't get you, there was always polio. Besides, the priest and the nuns at school were always there to remind you of eternal damnation (and how God would get you), so you were too worried about the next life to put a foot wrong in this one. Well that's if you were good. If you weren't good you would head for purgatory, or worse, limbo. Eileen thinks of the time her friend Ruth lifted every piece of heavy furniture in their small flat for a month, trying to get rid of a foetus she'd managed to grow inside her.

Religion had seemed to be all about secrets and choice: how to pick the right door, find the gold, the biggest dog, the magic tinderbox.

She stops dusting and looks at herself in the mirror, actually looks, as though looking at someone for the first time.

'Time to tell that husband of yours,' she says to her reflection. 'He needs to know, too. Even if he is a crank. And God knows you can't decide this one all on your own, girlie-girl.'

Right about now she feels nineteen years old, at the most; no matter how hard she looks, she can't reconcile the reflection she sees with what is going on inside of her. Grace, that's what she needs right now. Maybe she should stop taking her anti-epilepsy drugs, see if she can get God back; maybe He could help her decide what to do.

Colours were the first to change. Carmine flowers, yellow faces, a deep blue wash of stone. She would be filled with a heavy weight, like a gas-filled balloon had entered her chest, swelling slowly. And then the feeling would come, the one she waited for, hoped for. Emotion as melodic as Barber ever wrung out of his 'Adagio for Strings' would rush in; a swell of hope that she knew was God's own love seeded inside of her, and as she gave herself over to this seed she would connect with whatever she touched; if she wandered out into the garden and lay down amongst Gabriel's Douce Provence peas, she could touch them and feel them grow up and turn to face the sun, and she would feel herself grow towards the sun. If she happened to be in town when the aura started, she would stand in the middle of Shop Street, the shoppers and workers on their lunch breaks washing past her, she would reach out her arms, close her eyes and she would feel their air touching her skin, their heat joining the heat of her body. She considered each aura—episodes, Gabriel called them—a gift from God, a chance to experience the world as He had created it, suffused with love and wonder. And so she re-discovered God, re-claimed him from the faded chants of her convent schoolbooks and Latin masses, long after she had given up on the Church, and replaced the weekly rituals with catching the condom train to Belfast, newspaper deadlines, the calls of her two boys.

When the specialist told her these were simple partial seizures, she couldn't connect them to her brain, that lump of jelly inside her skull. When God came back, it felt as if there were more of her, and more of the world. Can a person discover God and lose him twice in one lifetime? She hasn't been able to figure that one out yet, so she's hanging onto things she can touch or do: the squishiness of fresh bread, Frasier's flank under the brush, her monthly book club, her morning salsa class down at the Gateway hotel—but if she doesn't believe in God, what will she believe in? She's given up putting any stock into herself, found herself to be too unreliable, wanting in the area of expansion.

LSD came after her time; she had only ever experimented with drugs when Ruth, a registered nurse, brought home a supply of prescription-only tablets to help them get through the late nights they had to work one winter, when the clouds dipped low over Dublin's rooftops and these two culchies from Galway knew they had to make it here or hit the boat.

Electrical activity in the brain, according to the specialist. Late-onset epilepsy, said she probably had a low seizure threshold, as if that would make sense of this new part of her life.

Eileen longs for clarity, for the sense of completeness she used to have, before she started on the medication, before her seizures changed. The specialist said this sometimes happened, that epileptic activity could continue while on certain treatment, but that as long as the seizures occurred less frequently, they would stick with this treatment. Sure enough, she only gets a couple a year now, nothing like the auras that used to visit her every month, like unexpected gifts. Eileen misses the sense of the fantastic, of possibility and inevitability that accompanied the auras, warnings of an impending seizure.

Now she just gets the low sadness that swells inside her. Most of all she dreads the seizures that start off at night, while she's asleep. Fear replaces the sadness, and small worries pile up on top of each other until she wakes up and feels as though she has swallowed something solid and heavy, a rock or a lead-lined ball. That Gabriel will forget to get the septic tank pumped out in time. That she will crash the car into that young mother who never looks before she turns out onto the main road, her three children sitting in the backseat, wearing their school uniforms. That no one will ever know that she once thumbed the entire length of the country, from Kenmare to Letterkenny.

And what to do about Frasier; the only worry she will have to share with Gabriel. Splinters, that's how she thinks of the rest of them, small glassy splinters scattered in her belly, her heart, her brain.

Of course, it means she shouldn't drive now. She gets away with it, she still has two years on her licence and anyway who would stop her, but she worries about what might happen. Though she thinks perhaps this worry is connected to her age and not the epilepsy at all; she has seen that same look of caution on the faces of the women her age shopping in Marks & Spencer, the way they reach out to steady themselves before they move away from the prepared chicken, baskets held out in front of them to stop people getting too close.

She corners Gabriel when he comes out of the bathroom, after his morning shave, before she can change her mind.

Eileen tells him that the vet wants them to have Frasier put down. *Put down*, that's the exact phrase she uses, and he heads straight out to the shed, doesn't say a word. She follows him outside, walks in concentric circles in the back garden, around and around past the winter pansies, afraid to follow him all the way into the shed, but afraid to be on her own in the house with Frasier and his brown intelligent eyes.

Gabriel has two hideaways; places he can go to get away from her now that neither of them is officially working. When they bought this four bedroom house down in County Galway—her idea to use his lump sum to retire back to her home place, though she never thought they would actually do it—far enough from town to forget the rat race that ploughed on without them, they divided up the rooms between them, staked their claim before they had even moved in. The master bedroom with the bathroom en-suite would be for the two of them to sleep in (they still slept together, in the same bed, unlike some couples she knew), the bedroom right next to it would be for visitors down from Dublin. She took the smaller of the two remaining bedrooms. She didn't care about the size, she just wanted it because it faced the road—she could set up her desk under the window and watch the road, look for signs of life.

Eileen doesn't use the room though. Whenever she picks up a stray editing job, she sets up at the kitchen table. Though she has spent a lifetime dodging housework and living on one large chicken casserole for a week, she still associates the kitchen with work, with real productivity.

Frasier hasn't followed her into the garden; he struggles even to walk as far as the back door, where she has set out a litter tray for him. And the poor boy has been using it, adapting like a cat, as far away from the temperamental and sensitive puppy as she can possibly imagine him being. It's gotten to the stage where she remembers what she calls his teenage stage—when he was all long legs and energetic muscle and appetite—fondly, the way he used to grab the ends of the couch covers, her cushions, the towels she'd hang out on the line, grabbing the ends of them in his strong jaws, ripping them to ribbons.

'We have to make this decision,' she calls out to Gabriel. 'It's up to us.'

And now she feels like a nag. A dithering one, at that.

From where she's standing, in the middle of her flattened grass circles, she hears the sound of hammering, loud and arrhythmic. Eileen almost goes over to the shed door, until something falls in there. It sounds like a box of nails.

To hell with him. She heads back inside, to the kitchen. Frasier is still waiting for them at the back door, ears cocked and tongue hanging out.

'What are you looking at,' she says to him. Then feels worse.

'Food is good,' Gabriel says to her, and she knows things are bad. They're eating a tuna pasta bake she has made with an out-of-date tin of tuna she found in the back of the press and a packet of cream of vegetable soup. She didn't even have any cheese to sprinkle over it; she spent the afternoon cleaning out the kitchen rather than going to Supervalu to pick up the weekly shop. Sometimes cleaning comes to her like this: after a fortnight of stacking the dirty dishes on the counter beside the sink and rinsing a plate or a mug as needed, she feels the need to impose order. It's the only time she likes cleaning, or can tolerate it, even. When the boys were still at home it was worse, she used to stack the dirty pots and pans on the floor, or just outside the back door if they had started to smell bad, shoving them into the oven if someone called over.

Frasier lies under the table, crunching on prime dog food enriched with fish oils and vitamin C, the dish set between his front paws.

The weight in Eileen's solar plexus is back. She has put on Mozart's 'Sonata for Two Pianos in D Major' to see if it will help. Frasier doesn't come over to nuzzle her hand, to warn her of the electrical surge about to start in her brain, his hips are so bad. He barked at her a lot this afternoon as she cleaned out the utility room, but she put it down to a longing to join in with the mop, didn't click until the heaviness came back that a seizure was on the way. Episodes, Gabriel still calls them. As if they are some sort of hysterical woman thing, specific to Eileen, whom he considers a creative type and therefore highly strung.

Gabriel used to work with other people's feet, he was a chiropodist with the Health Board; she used to think this grounded him, somehow. Now she knows he has his own modes of escape.

'So have you signed your organ donor card yet?' Eileen says across the table, to wake him up, get some sort of reaction from him. He looks up, his eyes wide and blank with the effort to not think about what comes before organ donation.

'No,' he says and looks back down at his plate, waves of discomfort radiating from him. Eileen left the card out for him over three weeks ago.

'Well, have you thought about what to do with Frasier?' She prods him, looking for a spark, though she herself has not had the will to contemplate bringing Frasier back to the vet. He lifts his tail in a slow thump thump thump when he hears his name.

'No,' he says and he looks up, anger and annoyance and fear plain on his face, in equal measures.

'Well I think we should both carry a donor card,' she says and already she is making plans to draw up a will, something neither of them has ever done, not even when the boys were around to worry about. For some reason, she finds it easier to consider her own mortality; certainly this is the first time she's been willing to admit that death will happen to her, too. She's getting old enough to know that she'll never be as wise as when she was four years old, the way she could challenge anyone in charge.

How come the decisions she has to make about another being's life still come as a surprise? As if someone has come along, taken her childlike self and said—now, decide what to do with Solomon's baby. It's a shock every time to be left with this crying, wriggling, slippery dilemma. *And I'm going to be sixty-eight in March, for heaven's sake.*

She doesn't tell people her age if she can help it, and tries not to think about terminal illness or accidents—she has good skin, dresses like a woman twenty years younger, and she doesn't want people treating her like an old lady. It's bad enough that her joints have started to stiffen all through the winter, that she gets these mysterious aches in her back, behind her lungs, without young people—a grouping that now includes her doctor, local chemist, police sergeant—treating her as though she is incompetent or invisible on grounds of her age. She has caught glimpses of herself in shop windows in the middle of January and wondered who that woman with the careful walk could be.

'And we'll have to make up a will,' she adds, just for distraction.

'I'm not sure I want to be a donor,' he says, and she knows he is choosing the subject that bothers him least, hoping this will get him off the hook for the others.

'When you're gone I'm going to donate your organs anyway. They'll be no use to you,' she tells him. 'Besides, it's not like you'll be able to do anything about it.'

He laughs, a bit hesitantly, that annoying way he has when he's not sure if she's winding him up. She wants him to change everything, or at least shout at her. And then she looks under the table, at Frasier licking the last of the food from his bowl, and she wonders, do the dead have rights, any more than the living?

Gabriel emerges from the shed with a trophy: he has built a foot-wide shallow box out of scraps of plywood, and on the sides of this, he has attached wheels. He's wearing his blue baseball hat, the one Matt brought over from Minnesota, the one he knows she detests. He has a determined look she hasn't seen since he hijacked her vague whim to retire to Galway.

'What's that?'

'You'll see,' he says, and she can tell he doesn't want to break the spell. Whatever he's up to, he doesn't want her tuppence worth. Or, she thinks, two cents worth.

'I'm going to the shop,' she tells him. Time to stock up, they ran out of loo roll two days ago and they have almost used up their last box of tissues. Time to get out of the house for a while. Time to pull a row of silk scarves from a bright blue hat, a swirling decision, a chance.

Frasier is trying his best to stay close to her. Must be more electrical activity. He's breaking her heart, small jagged pieces of brown mirror eyes splitting it, bit by bit, whenever she sees him climbing up into that ridiculous contraption Gabriel has made. Frasier is oblivious though, he cautiously places his front paws in first, the way Gabriel taught him, then sort of walks his hind legs in, slipping one front paw out the front at a time, replacing it with a back paw until he can settle his hips down into the small cart, and wheel himself along with his front legs. Eileen almost bends down to help him in, but she holds back; his dignity seems wrapped up in each careful movement, the careful placement of each limb. She wishes he would stop following her, trying to care for her. The guilt is wearing her out.

Eileen marvels at how little she can say to Gabriel if she concentrates: have you closed the bedroom window, I've already fed Frasier, if you see the postman will you give him this. Nothing else, no adornments.

So far, they haven't had a conversation since she raised the organ donor card issue.

Frasier's water dish is empty, he's licking the last few drops from the bottom of it—Eileen reaches down to take the bowl at the same moment as Gabriel does; her hand pauses on soft flank, his hand on the other side, the two of them joined by warm blood, flesh, soft fur.

The silence she has surrounded herself with makes every movement and word stand out. She notices Gabriel's reaction when the vet phones to see has she decided, and would she like an appointment. Gabriel is angry, yes. But it's more than just that—it's another man ringing her, on their phone. Or maybe he thinks of it as his phone, she doesn't know. It's territorial, anyway, whatever is bothering him.

Staying quiet makes him easier to deal with. And who knows, maybe she'll hear what she needs to. Find some answers in the ether.

Eileen walks out into the garden with Frasier, it's almost an hour since he lapped up a bowl of vitamin C enriched water, and he has asked to go out. She walks out as far as the crocuses blooming in the low sunlight, turns away from the sight of Frasier, only seven years old and barely able to lift his leg up, pee dribbling down the inside of his leg, steam rising from his damp fur. She enters Gabriel's shed, piles up every unfinished project from his bench into her arms, dropping a turned end-table leg just outside the shed door. In the centre of the back garden, she arranges the jumble of wood and part-assembled joints on the dormant grass.

HERE I AM.

In clumsy stick letters, she has spelt it out. All she needs now is the barbeque lighter fluid.

Frasier's sixth sense must be at work—he hobbles over to her and sits down beside her, leaning up against her shin. She stays perfectly still, afraid that if she moves he might move away. Together, they look ahead, over the stretch of tended grass, past the pile of mud spilling out of the base of the compost bin, at the red leafless stems of the dogwood, quiet and stiff in the winter cool, the flash of purple from the winter hardy violas, the splayed rhododendron leaves, defying geography to settle wildly amongst the bog grass that springs up in sodden corners. A murmuration of starlings sweeps down to the tops of the mountain ash, swerving up to their expanse of sky, and Eileen reflexively looks up at the back windows. Gabriel is standing at his window, looking down on them both, his body a blur of blue behind the winter-scuffed pane. The streaks that run down the glass mix with her view of him, and all of a sudden it's as if she can see him up close: the tears streaming down his cheeks, dripping off his chin onto the window, running out through the glass to her face, her cheeks dripping, and the three of them are mixing together, slipping out of this world, merging into fluid colours: cobalt blue and green, burnt umber, the colours of the earth and the sky swimming through Eileen and Gabriel and Frasier, the three of them touching, close, their molecules intermingling in this safe place; warm fluid, colours darkening, where she knows their spirits begin.

RISING SLOWLY

Maeve puts down her cup of coffee—a black Americano—and props her chin in her hands. Paper carrier bags litter the floor around her feet. Orla's taking forever in the toilets, and it's not long until closing time. Daydream time.

Orla hefts the handbag off the other chair so she can sit down. 'Jeezus, Maeve, what have you got in here—a dead body?'

'Careful, that's an Isabella Fiore!' The waiter mops the floor nearby, and Maeve makes a half-hearted attempt to shove her shopping out of his way.

'Always a bag lady, hunh, Maeve. I remember when you used to empty the contents of your handbag in the middle of the living room floor before going out so you could decant all the important stuff into a clutch.'

'Yeah. Still doing it, every Friday night ...'

'Me and Helen used to nick bits and pieces when you weren't looking—lip-gloss, loose earrings, even tampons. Hide them in our school bags to show off on Monday morning. Maeve treasure.'

'And there all that time I thought I had fairies. Or that the stuff in my handbag was going to the same place as odd socks.'

A phone rings, playing the first few bars of 'Jailhouse Rock'. Maeve roots through her pockets, pulls out loads of stuff—crumpled tissues, keys, a pink lace bra with the tags still on it, a pair of yellow knickers with the tag attached—and dumps it all on the table. No sign of her phone.

Orla lifts the lace bra by its edge. 'Where did you get this?'

'Dunnes, I think.' Maeve focuses on stirring two packets of sugar into her coffee.

'I didn't see you buying them.'

'Well. They were just sitting there. So I thought, why not?'

'Why not what?'

'Slip them into my bag.'

'What? You mean you nicked them?'

'Don't worry, no one was looking.'

Orla closes her eyes, speaks quietly. 'I won't say a word. No. Not a word.'

Maeve removes a lipstick from her jeans pocket and pulls the seal off. 'Yeah well, you were with me. So that makes you an accessory.'

'Put that lipstick away! It's stolen, isn't it?'

'Oh relax for heavensake, who went and made you my keeper? What used Helen say—you're not the boss of me?'

They stare at the pile of stuff Maeve has dumped in the middle of the table. The only other customer in the place goes to the counter to order a take-away coffee.

Orla sorts the packets of sugar into two piles, brown sugar and white, and puts them back into opposite sides of the same bowl. 'It was nice, what that priest said at the mass, about Helen's passing being a new beginning. I feel like she's still here with me, you know?'

'Well, I guess that's one way to look at it. I don't know why he had to comment on the fact she didn't have kids though. Like that was all there was to her—something she didn't have. And let's face it, it's just as well she didn't—as if the world needs more messed-up children.'

'Still, it'd be nice to have kids, wouldn't it? I mean, for even one of us to. I thought Helen would be the one, of all of us, but—'

'But she went and married that bollocks Brendan. And thank God he never reproduced.'

'Yeah, could you imagine—stingy little number-crunchers whingeing in their little brown jumpers ...'

Orla's mobile phone rings, the default Nokia tune. She takes it out of her pocket and looks at the screen. 'His ears must be burning—yes hello. Oh hi Brendan. Sure, what is it? No, still haven't come across them. And you've checked the whole house? What about the car? Right so.' Orla hangs up on him, then holds the phone out in front of her. 'Well, jeezus if you cared so bloody much why did you leave them there on the kitchen table then?' She shakes her head and sips some of the milk froth from her cappuccino. 'I still can't believe he's lost her ashes. Helen's ashes! Not even a month after the funeral.'

'The waster.' Maeve pulls a pair of glittery socks out of the top of her bag and starts to take one of her shoes off.

'Jeezus Maeve, did you nick those socks too? Leave them back into your bag, will you. You're not going to change your socks here in the middle of the café, are you? You haven't changed a bit, not since we were kids. Imagine what Helen would say.'

Both women are quiet for a moment, lost in their own thoughts. Maeve puts on one sock but drops the other one onto the table.

Orla leans her face on her hands. 'I keep talking to Helen, asking her things. Like is this guy the one or is he another one wasting time. As if she's died and turned into God or something ... I like that idea though. She would have made a good God.'

'No, she'd be too soft,' Maeve says. 'She'd put up with too much. Look at that husband of hers, what she had to put up with.'

'The fecker. I wish he had buried her properly. I'd like to visit her grave. Have somewhere to go to talk to her, remember her. I guess there's not much left here for us anymore.'

'Mmm. No real reason to come back.'

'Remember the Christmas Mum and Dad were fighting so bad, Dad threatening to leave again, and the three of us hid under the tree? How Helen told us that enchanted gnomes lived in Christmas trees waiting to trap children and gobble them up? So we were too frightened to stay under the tree and too frightened to get out …'

'Mmm.'

'The way she could tell a joke or a scary story and make us forget whatever was going on …'

'Mm-hmmm.'

'Oh come on. You could at least pretend to be listening.'

'Look, you know I'm not into all that sentimental crap.'

'I'm not being sentimental—what's wrong with looking back? I want to remember. The good things, the shite, whatever. And feck you Miss Independent over from your busy life in London.'

'Stall the ball there, missy. Far as I remember, you ran off to Dublin years ago. Didn't hear you crying.'

'But don't you miss home? With Mum dead, and Helen now too. And Dad fecking off to live in Portugal—'

'Oh come on, Galway hasn't been home since Mum died. Even when Helen was still alive. I mean, Mum was home, you know. The city, well, it's just another place. Yeah sure, I have as many cosy memories of the place as I have grim ones, but—it's just streets and shops and other people's houses.'

'And Helen's home.'

'What do you want from me? At least I came back over for her Month's Mind! Besides, I've done my bit for Helen.'

Orla waves her cup at the stolen garments in the middle of the table. Coffee slops over the rim. 'Yeah, by nicking stuff, you klepto.'

'Like you've never broken the law, Miss New-Goody-Two-Shoes. I remember what you got up to in college, the stories you used to tell me. You've seen enough—'

'Yeah well, this is different.'

'You listen to too many chat shows. How to live a better life in thirty seconds. Feck that.'

Orla stops mopping up the spilt coffee. 'Oh for—'

'Look Orla, I know—I know I seem a bit ... But not everyone's like you. So leave it alone, will you? Just leave it ... I swear I could kill Helen. You know, if she was here.'

Orla reaches her hand out to her sister, but doesn't quite touch her. 'It's strange, isn't it, since she died—'

Maeve's phone rings. Da-dum. Da-dum. She ignores it. It rings again, the opening bars of 'Jailouse Rock' grinding over and over. She opens her handbag and looks inside, pushing things around. 'Where is that phone? No matter how many times I clean out my bag, the rubbish seems to find its way back in. What is it with handbags?' Maeve empties everything out onto the table piece by piece. 'Do they collect the leftover bits and pieces from the entire world and store them up just in case? Wouldn't it be great if there was a handbag that could hold everything you ever needed, but open it up and whatever you asked for would rise to the top?' She places two more stolen yellow thongs on the table, and the phone goes quiet. 'I don't even wear thongs. If I don't want visible panty line I don't wear knickers. And now I've got four thongs. In yellow.'

'I miss her, you know.'

'I know.'

'I was closer to her than you were. We were friends.'

'I know.'

'Why did she have to go and die, Maeve? Why Helen?'

Maeve is distracted by the phone ringing. She removes a stolen scarf and a pair of sunglasses from her almost-empty handbag. 'Well, you know what they say about cancer, one in three will get it. I guess that leaves the two of us safe enough—drink, smoke, steal all the shite you want—'

'How can you joke about that? Our sister is dead, don't you get it? Dead. Gone. For good. So start acting like a normal person would.'

'I'm trying, but—'

'But?'

'But—you didn't even tell me how bad she was. You told me she was out of the hospital and I thought she was getting better, not dying. You should have told me how bad she'd got, Orla. You should have said something.'

Maeve finally finds the ringing phone, puts her bag on the table, and turns away from Orla. 'Hello Maeve's phone. Oh hi Brendan. No. Un-unh, still no sign of her. Yeah okay, I'll let you know if I come across them.'

The waiter comes over to clear away their cups, and Orla lifts the handbag off the table. It's heavy; she swings it over to her lap. 'So what's in this bag any—'

'Don't!' Maeve tries to grab the bag, but her sister pulls away, just out of reach.

'Maeve, what's this?' Orla lifts up a metal canister.

'Uh ...'

'You've been carrying *this* around in your handbag?'

'Uh ...'

'Jeezus, you haven't been carrying Helen around in your handbag all weekend, have you?'

Maeve grabs the container of ashes from Orla and hugs it to her chest. She whimpers and makes a funny face so she looks like a child.

'What were you thinking Maeve? Honestly!'

'Well—well, there wasn't a chance in hell I was leaving her with Brendan. For God's sake, the guy arranged a cremation without even *talking* to us. No way I was leaving Helen behind. Not with that bollocks. He treated her bad enough when she was alive, no way could I leave her there. You know, what's left of her.'

'So you nicked her ashes?'

'They were just sitting there, on the kitchen table, looking at me. Well, the urn was.'

'So you nicked her ashes.'

Maeve nods. The two of them burst out laughing.

'Jeezus, Maeve. You're something else.'

'I didn't know what to do—Mum's gone, and now Helen's gone, and I just wanted to hang on to a piece of her ... to be with her somehow. I thought maybe I'd go down the prom, empty her ashes into the surf, let the Atlantic take her away.' They both look out the window at the rough sea. Low clouds seem as though they are breaking up against the wave tips. 'But, now I don't know. I think I want to keep her.'

Orla takes the urn and places it in the bottom of Maeve's handbag. They start to move the contents of Maeve's bag from the table, piling stolen knickers and crumpled tissues and old till receipts on top of Helen's ashes. 'Too bad Helen wasn't here to see this.'

'Yeah.'

Orla reaches across the table and takes her sister's hand. 'She would have killed you, Maeve. She would have fecking killed you.'

TELLING STORIES

Mum was talking in her sleep again. She'd been doing it ever since we left Dad. I could never make out what she was saying.

'Just ignore her, Bernadette. Let me finish my story.' Esmay sat on the end of my bed with a book on her lap, just out of reach. Her small frame was stooped and withered. The streetlights reflected off her black-rimmed glasses as she found the place she had stopped reading the night before.

'Hmmm, right. Here we are now … And then the little red-haired girl called Bernadette,' Esmay read, glancing up at me, 'felt herself being lifted by the strong wind. She knew she was being punished for being a wicked little girl. But she didn't know the wind would carry her far, far away …'

The story continued while I tried to ignore Esmay, hoping if I didn't look at her, she'd go away. I stuck my fingers in my ears, but I could still hear her. Mum didn't know about Esmay. I didn't want to tell her, in case Esmay started to visit her too. Mum knew about my other friends, though, the ones I left behind. She called them figments of my imagination. She said they weren't real.

Esmay never visited during the day, when I was doing things. That's why I didn't spend much time in bed. Mum always let me stay up late with her. She said she needed the company. I had the place to myself in the mornings, though.

I was already drinking sweet tea in the kitchen when Mum poked her head around the door. 'Oh, so that's where you are, Ber. I was wondering where you'd got to.' Her eyes were red and sunk into her head. She looked as though she had been crying.

I got up to switch the kettle back on. 'Fancy a cuppa tea?' I thought she might need one.

'Mmmm. Maybe I'll have a strong one. Bring it upstairs for me, will you, Ber.' A strong one meant I was to put a capful of Johnny Powers into it. She said it helped to clear her head after a bad night's sleep.

I brought the tea up to Mum. She was back in bed. She started telling me about her bad dreams. I pretended to listen, nodding my head and saying 'mmm-hmm' in the right places. I only paid attention to her when she started to talk about Dad.

'You don't know the whole story, what it was like, Ber.' Mum leaned forward in the bed, the sunshine picking out the grey hairs on her blonde head. 'Your father was a difficult man to live with. But that's all in the past now.'

These three lines were in every rant about Dad, mixed in with stories about the things they used to get up to together. How mad they once were. And how it had all changed. He had never really loved her and never would. She was shocked they had managed to have me, even. Her immaculate conception, she called me. She would start out calling Dad by his name and end up referring to him as 'your father'. As though I had something to do with it, the change in him. As though somehow he was mine.

Before I went downstairs, I convinced Mum to pay me fifty pence to unpack some of the boxes in the kitchen.

The day we moved into the flat Mum had been overtaken by a cleaning frenzy. 'C'mon Ber, let's make this place our own. You'd never know what germs the last people here left behind.'

We had walked up to the shop to buy some Domestos, up the laneway and past the payphone where all the kids in the area gathered. They made fun of us because I was holding Mum's hand. I turned ten last June, but Mum still liked me to hold her hand. 'It makes me feel safe,' she would say.

By the time we got home, Mum had lost interest in cleaning. She claimed she only had enough energy to mop the kitchen floor. 'C'mere and help me with these boxes, Ber. Then we can have a tea break.'

So we sorted out the boxes according to their contents and left them in the middle of the right room. Then Mum stretched out on the couch with a cup of tea and I spent the rest of the day reading the problem pages of Mum's magazines. We were to live out of boxes for a while yet.

After I had unpacked the rest of the pots and pans, I snuck outside with my fifty-p piece. Mum was asleep. I didn't like to wake her. She got jumpy when we moved here.

The street was empty. The local children weren't allowed to play outside on the street. The area didn't have a good reputation, but Mum said it was cheap. Anyway, at lunchtime most people were inside eating. There were still a few teenagers clustered in the laneway, constantly shifting.

'Hey culchie girl, where's your Mammy today? Would ya like me to hold your hand so ya don't get scared?' shouted a boy wearing dark blue jeans and bright white running shoes. He always set the rest of them off.

I just held my head up high and called them names in my head. Neanderthals. Insignificant worms. Amoeba-brains. Probably couldn't understand polysyllabic words. Hold your head up and ignore them. But by the time I turned the corner at the top of the lane I was sweating and my hands were shaking. I would never let it show, though. I would never let them know how much I hated walking up that laneway.

The phone box was just outside the shop. The last three times I had been to the phone, I had hung up before Dad could answer the phone. I had spent the twenty pence on Taytos instead. Crisps were never allowed in the house before. Dad said they were junk, not fit for human consumption. We weren't allowed to go to McDonalds either.

It was hot inside the phonebox. I checked the receiver for gunge. The local gurriers frequently smeared sticky stuff on the mouthpiece. It was safe today though. On weeknights the teenagers were called in early, it was weekends they did most damage.

I put the fifty pence piece in the slot. I didn't want to have to ask for change from the shopkeeper. He was nosy. A gossip, Mum called him. She went to him anytime she needed to know anything, like where to get cheap shoes. Or what all the racket on Thursday night was about. I paused before dialling the last digit. I didn't even have to try to remember the number, it seemed like a piece of me. A piece I had left behind.

I wasn't sure if I wanted to talk to Dad. I didn't know what I would say.

We had left in a hurry, Mum and myself. I had left a lot of stuff behind in the flurry of packing that filled the days before we left. Mum had been threatening to leave for ages. None of us believed she was finally going through with it. I think even Mum was surprised to find herself in a new home, in the city.

Mum regularly reminded me of our agreement, the one we had made on the way up to the city. 'It's to be a total blackout. No contact with your father whatsoever. The past is the past and we are leaving it behind us. If he wants to carry on like that it's his business. I won't have any of it.'

So I had to make sure she didn't find out about this, these trips to the payphone. I kept an eye on the laneway. I let the phone ring six times, two rings longer than the last time.

'Hello?' A man answered, but it wasn't Dad's voice. I didn't know what to say. I didn't want anyone to know I was calling, just Dad. 'Hello? Is anyone there?'

I put the phone down slowly and gently, and held the phonebox door so it wouldn't slam shut. My hands were clammy. I kept walking, counting off each crack in the pavement as I stepped on it. I was on sixty-three by the time I got to the front door.

My hands had returned to normal but I couldn't even remember passing by the boys in the lane on the way back. I slipped inside, closing the door softly behind me so I wouldn't wake Mum.

That night was a restless one. Mum was feeling nervous, so we sat up trying on clothes and picking out the things we'd like to buy from the stack of catalogues Mum had collected. Mum was using her bedroom as a walk-in closet since she was sleeping in mine. When we finally got to bed, Mum crashed out and started snoring loudly.

I couldn't sleep. Esmay was back. She held a book open with one hand, and patted her stiff dark hair with the other hand. Esmay was telling me another story. 'And you see, the lady in black could read the little girl's thoughts. She knew the little girl had been scheming treacherous plans. The little girl thought she was so clever. But the lady in black knew the little girl had been thinking of ways to hurt her, to get rid of her. She knew that if she didn't act soon, the little girl would abandon her …'

Esmay looked up, smiling at me in the dim light. My hands blocked my ears, and my eyes and mouth were scrunched up tightly. She knew I could still hear her, though, and that I could still see her. She knew there was nothing I could do to block her out. So she continued her story. 'The lady in black spent weeks and months hatching her plans for the little girl. All the while, the wicked little girl suspected nothing of this. All the while, the wicked little girl thought things which were not private at all ...'

Mum shook me awake later that night. It was still dark out. Her eyes were wide and glassy. 'Where's my holy water? Where did you put it?'

'I dunno,' I mumbled. I tried to turn over but she grabbed my shoulder.

'And my Blessed Virgin, what did you do with her?'

I sat up and told her that I hadn't unpacked either of them. She was rubbing her bottom lip with her thumb. Back and forth. Back and forth. Not a good sign.

'Well then, what happened to them? Did your father take them from me?'

That was enough to get me out of bed. I knew she wouldn't let go if she thought Dad was to blame. I had to find that statue. I took her by the hand and led her downstairs.

'Thanks Bernadette,' said Mum. She rarely called me by my full name. Saint Bernadette of Lourdes was my namesake. Mum prayed to Our Lady of Lourdes daily, even though she wasn't religious in any other way. I don't remember her going to Mass, except at Easter. She liked the notion of rebirth.

Dad didn't believe in God, though. Not since I can remember, anyway. He said it was a load of guff. Mum said he used to be a Catholic, until after I was born.

Mum pulled on the blonde hairs at the nape of her neck and hovered over me as I went through the boxes in the living room. I thought I had found the BVM when I saw the candles in one of the boxes. Mum had always kept a tidy little shrine for her Blessed Virgin Mary statue, with several white candles she lit each day while she prayed. I tore apart the boxes in the dining room, but there was no sign of either the BVM or the holy water.

'I'll say a prayer to Saint Anthony,' Mum said, by way of helping me.

Finally I spied a little blue head sticking out of a box in the downstairs toilet. However it had gotten there. 'Found it,' I hollered over my shoulder. I brought the whole box back to the living room, where Mum had already started assembling her shrine. The coffee table was now covered with the good linen tablecloth, and the candles had been placed in a semi-circle.

'C'mere to me, don't be so slow, give me that box, Ber.' Mum dug out a bottle of holy water and sprinkled some over the table, before carefully placing the BVM in the centre. She touched the small figure reverentially, as if it possessed special power.

To me it just looked ugly. The blue paint had bled from the veil onto the orange painted face. The hands had chipped in transit, and the white robes had yellowed long ago from Dad's cigarette smoking. But at least Mum was calm now. I could go back to bed. I kissed the top of her head as she leant forward to light the candles. 'Goodnight Mum.'

Mum looked up briefly. 'Oh, goodnight Ber,' she said, her voice steady and light. 'And thanks. We should have done this ages ago, when we first moved in. Things would have been much better for us.'

I nodded and went upstairs to bed.

It was early on Saturday morning and no one in the area was out of bed yet. I hadn't slept at all that night. Esmay paid a visit, but she didn't stay for long. She said she had other things to do. I just tossed and turned all night.

I remember when I was younger, Dad used to tell me stories when I couldn't sleep. He used to call me his little monkey. But as he argued more with Mum, he talked less to me.

Mum must have fallen asleep on the couch. For the first time since we moved here, almost three weeks ago now, I had the room to myself. But still I couldn't sleep. By eight o'clock I gave up trying and slipped out of the flat, clutching Mum's change purse in my hand. She would never notice the difference.

The laneway seemed brighter in the early morning light. It was quiet, and it smelled like piss. My tummy was quivering. I felt like I was going to throw up.

'I'm going to ring Dad. I'm going to ring my Dad.' I kept repeating this to myself, over and over, just a whisper, barely audible.

'I'm going to ring Dad. I'm going to ring Dad.' All the way to the phone box, I kept whispering this.

I dialled my home number, pressing each number carefully, still whispering to myself between each digit. I froze when the phone started to ring out. Four rings. Five rings. Six rings. Ten rings and still no answer. It was Saturday morning, early. I let it ring on. As I was counting the thirteenth ring, it stopped.

'Hello?' It was Dad's voice this time, definitely Dad. His voice sounded muffled and confused. 'Hello?' he repeated. I had probably woken him.

I opened my mouth, but I didn't know what to say. The mouthpiece was sticky. Dad, I kept thinking, Dad.

'I miss you,' I whispered as I squeezed my eyes shut, blocking everything else out. I didn't know if he could hear me. I couldn't talk any louder. I couldn't say anything more. It was too quiet outside.

The phone line was clear and silent. I tried to think of what he looked like. I wanted to hear his voice.

'Ber, is that you?' he finally whispered, as though there was someone else listening in.

THE GOOD BOAT

Eight girls heft oars onto shoulders. They walk out, one by one, oars pointing towards the water. A crew of boys watches them, and the girls can feel their gaze on the backs of their white T-shirts, half curiosity, half contempt. Lustful looks stopped after the girls' warm-up: ten minutes of flexibilities, five minutes running on the spot inside the boat shed.

The boys are one man short of a row up the river, left hanging around the slip watching their boat being held down by a girl. The girls place their oars across the gunnels, clunk clunk clunk by eight. One of them curses. 'Don't hit me with that oar, Catriona.'

Jo, their coach, buzzes around, hushing storms. The boys are watching.

The boat is ready for them; the girls slip their feet into the boat's toughened shoes and fit their oars into the oarlocks. They know what they're doing, but it feels different in the good boat. It feels good to sense the boys' discontent.

Push off with the oars and off they go, away from the weir, around

Friar's Cut and aim up towards Menlo Castle, synchronicity, the white boat sitting up level and all the blades feathering in unison, a flat skim through the cold air just above the water. They move up the slides smoothly. Drop and pull, and the force of their backs and thighs and forearms propels the boat through the brown water, grey skies and raindrops forgotten.

Jo cycles along the riverbank shouting corrections at the top of her voice. Some of the boys' first crew are watching them; if the boat is to sit level on the water they must move with perfect unity. Concentrate. This is their first row out of the wooden boat (known as The Coffin). *Xavier II*, the good boat proclaims on its glossy side. This boat is only two years old and today the girls will glide in fibreglass, soar through the water like a swan.

A launch threatens to upset the boat with a wash; their cox calls, 'Ease up!'

Mick's orange megaphone—really a stolen traffic cone with either end sliced off—pushes out the four words that cut through the noise of the launch's motor, the sound of blood rushing past ears. 'Okay bring it back!'

Eighth boy found, and it's the first crew's boat. The girls know they will have to turn around at the Iodine. They know they are still being watched, so they row a hard ten, aim for unity.

Back at the boathouse, wood is for second crews and girls.

*

Race day. The nine teenage girls gather next to the gaping side of the boathouse in a circle around Coach. She's wearing her lucky hat today, the one her father wore in Rhodesia. 'Five minutes warm-up,' she calls, spots the boys' crews shifting around the slip, getting ready for their fours race. 'Inside!' she tells the girls, and they all move around to make sure that Helen is running on the spot with her back to the water so the boys can't gawk at her large breasts.

The girls start their flexibilities—three repetitions of each stretch—and Coach gives her pep talk, reminds them of strategy. This will be the last Head of the River this winter. The last river-long race by time trial. First race at home, though. Their usual days cling to them like shadows, and they line out along the good boat, theirs for the next half hour.

'Right, let's get this right.' Coach doesn't need to say this out loud, the words waft off the tense line of her shoulders, through the thick woolly overcoat she salvaged from the men's section of Anthony Ryan's. Her mouth is a thin slit.

Alongside the boat, the girls become their positions. Cox saves her venom for the bus-ride home to Furbo, back to the house where she's not allowed to get things wrong. She keeps the good words for the boat, hollers them from her belly. 'Hands on, ready to lift, and lift!' And they edge the boat out of the top rack.

'Ready and down to shoulders.' The girls lower the boat to their shoulders, opposite their rigger, a steady walk out, led by Cox. The boat hovers above their shoulders, their steps in unison, the weight of other days still with them, crowding in the space between the shell of the boat and their heads.

Stroke carries the fading image of her German grandfather (from her first memories), her longing for the boy who sits across from her in Accountancy class.

Seven wishes she could ignore the possibility of losing, the knowledge she carries from the moment she gets out of bed that she will never be good enough, no matter what her little sister in the stern of the boat says.

Six carries the fear that her boyfriend wants to break up with her, again.

Five carries an extra stone and a special liking for West Coast Cooler, the freedom it brings.

Four brings the dark smudges under her eyes from her early morning chambermaid shifts before school, the guilt from missing training when she can't swap shifts.

Three holds onto dreams of beauty, of her long mousy hair turning blonde, of her joined-up freckles fading to perfect skin, of her four younger brothers turning into frogs.

Two brings her black nail polish and her cropped black hair, and makes up names for the coach (today she's Contracepta), pretends that her father is dead and not just missing in action.

Bow carries the flash temper that simmers below her skin, the same temper her mother lets boil over.

They reach the slip, turn so that the boat is alongside the water's edge.

'And up and over,' Cox calls. Coach watches every move of their coordinated limbs, their maroon and white backs. They lift the boat over their heads, tilt it down past their shoulders in one smooth movement, then pause, their knuckles white over the gunnels, and plop it gently into the water.

Coach takes Four aside, she's got a leak and she's got sixty seconds to change into shorts that don't show crimson on them—and yes her blue training shorts will have to do.

Butterflies tingle their bellies. The girls climb in, this is it, their chance to prove themselves. They're the last boat in the club to leave the slip and head up the river to the staggered start. Coach calls out one last bit of encouragement, then swings her leg over the crossbar on her bicycle, belts it over to the new bridge, the best vantage point for the finish line.

Stroke sets a slow rate and Cox stays quiet for most of the way up. They listen to the oars skim the surface of the water, the headwind blow past their ears, the birds in the reeds at Friar's Cut.

At Menlo Castle the boat starts to quiver. Cox has been saving her voice for this moment. 'Okay, settle down now, keep it easy. Only 4,350 metres from the lake to the finish. Just over sixteen minutes of your hardest rowing ever. Then you can fall over. Keep your head, your technique. Keep it easy! This race is ours.'

Ease up and drop. Bowside first, then strokeside joins in and they row the boat around in a small, choppy arc to the far side of the starting launch. They look at the end of their oars, the back of the girl in front of them, the tops of their socks. Anywhere but at the crew of nine girls waiting for the next slot behind them, waiting for a chance to row against the stopwatch, strike a winning time. They pretend theirs is the only boat in the world.

Up the slides, time to get ready, oars squared in the water at the catch, the point the oars will start to move the boat. Look straight ahead, not a breath—go—and they push with every cell of their being, their backs locked off, power shifting from foot to thigh to back to arm to oar, and the bow lifts out of the water, momentum, a surge through their blood as they float up the slides in measured unison. The boat slows beneath them, they catch the river in their oars and pull through the water, power, each stroke building speed, tailwind shifts and they soar past the slip at Menlo, oblivious to the reeds on the bend, water sounds—chook, shoomp, phwoosh—smooth movements, synchronised breath, catch, drive and feather, inhale on the recovery, slide and their weight shifts up the boat with the steady pulse of eight girls who know what's expected of them and who still find time to train between class and homework, who ignore the silence from the boys' crews, surrender themselves to the single movement, unity, putting every bit of themselves, every bit of longing, every bit of family friction, the overwrought teenage hormones, and Cox is calling the words they need to hear, Coach embodied in her voice—'Six don't push the rate, keep it steady, your boyfriend can't see you now'—one more thing to let go of, slipping away down the curved river, perfect technique and strong thighs—'don't lose it now, a hard ten, only 500 metres to go, and *one* forget the boys who don't see you, *two* forget your mum's new boyfriend, *three* forget your fucked-up family, *four* forget your secrets, *five* row with the bit of you that's going to fail Chemistry, *six* row for everyone else in this boat, *seven* row for yourself, *eight* no one is watching you now, *nine* no one else cares, *ten* row as though you have no tomorrow.'

And they do, they pull the boat as if they have nothing left but muscle and skin and sweat, they lift that boat out of the water, ragged breaths and ribs, and for sixteen minutes and thirty-four seconds they become perfect.

100 metres to the finish; the girls allow their gaze to slip, to imagine how the other crew has buckled under the weight of these cast-off troubles, the taste of another eight conflicts slowing the bow, moving down the boat, minutes behind.

'Take it home!' Cox hollers and they row their last ounce, rowing against the boys who want them to give up the good boat, against the teachers who want them to study more, against their mothers' worry that they'll damage themselves, against the lack of expectation that perfection, for them, will ever be achieved in the white polycarbonate hull of a rowing boat.

They row—sweat and grip and not enough lungs—and the boat is good.

They row home, to promises of parties, first pints, the kissing of boys, the shift to high heels and pointy-toe shoes.

INDUCE

Fare thee well
My own true love
Farewell for a while

I keep looking out for her—Mam I mean—expecting her to be spinning round the blind bend in her green Nissan Micra. Her Green Machine. I still look for her when I leave my dirty breakfast dishes on the coffee table, listen out for her reprimand. And I keep referring to her in the present tense, which I can tell is starting to annoy people. I get looks saying, you're cracked, but I'll let it go since your mother is only just buried. They think that because she died, she doesn't exist for me anymore. I don't know. I can almost see her when I am pottering around the house. Just out of the corner of my eye, when I bend down to pick up the stack of turf she left outside the back door, just in case. 'It can get cold in May, you know,' she used to say. Always watching out for frost.

Jimmy has threatened to light a fire under my bed. He figured nothing else would get me out of it. But interfering neighbours aren't as scary a prospect as being induced. I have heard some horror stories. According to the midwife, a hot curry, rampant sex, and walking were the only home remedies I could try. I hate curry. Tony and Donal haven't come to see me since I took to the bed, cowards that they are. The third trimester killed off the appeal I used to have for boys. So sex is out of the question. Walking is all I can try. Twenty-three years of age going on twenty-four, back in college and I can't drink, smoke or get anyone to shag me. So I'm heading out onto the low road, see how far I get. All I can think of is the first three lines of a song Mam used to sing me to sleep with. It's an old song, traditional. I can't remember the rest of the lyrics, so the first lines just circle around in my head, slipping out at the oddest times. Mary Black's voice singing them, instead of my mother.

When I try my legs out for the first time in three weeks, I almost give up before I reach the front door. I carry my large belly as far as the cherry tree, the blossoms falling steadily to the ground. I'm out of breath now, my breathing shallow from the baby pushing up against my ribcage. It will take me at least ten minutes to waddle home, twice as long as it took me to reach this tree.

I'm going away
But I'll return
If I go 10,000 miles

'Are you going back to college after the baby's born, after the summer?' Jimmy asks me when he catches me out the back, both of us hanging out our washing. Even the birds stop to hear the answer to that one. I've got a lot of cleaning to do, so I keep moving. He's getting used to being ignored.

I want to go back to bed. I want that comfort, the warm smell of worn bedding, my childhood room. But now that I'm up, I can't stop doing. Sleep isn't happening for me and there's nothing I can take to help, not with the baby still inside. I'm in a fog. A clean-the-kitchen, hoover-the-corners-of-the-living-room, busy kind of fog.

But I still haven't cleaned out Mam's room. I don't want to air out her smells. I don't want to tidy up her bits and pieces, the last things her hands touched. Her Estée Lauder compact, Sr. Stanislaus' *Seasons of the Day: a Book of Hours*, a framed black and white photo of her parents. I want to keep all of her that I can.

I come into her room to sit, late at night when Killaguile is sleeping. I sit on her bed, hands on my belly, not touching anything. She's here. About to walk in any minute now. I can feel her in the dim glow the security light casts into the room. She fills this room, leaves just enough space for me to sit on the edge of her bed. And the baby.

'I'll watch out for you both,' she said before the pain and the morphine got too strong for thought or clear speech. 'Mind you get that child a father,' she had to add. As though respectability had become a sudden priority.

I lower myself down the front step, my walk for the day. I'll have to coax this baby to move out. Threatening doesn't seem to help. I get into a rhythm, my hips rolling to get my legs to walk. Today I will get past the cherry tree. More lines of Mam's lullaby swirl around my mind, Mary Black singing them straight from her mid-eighties *Collected* album. Not Mam's low version. I still can't hear her voice.

At the bottom of the garden I meet up with a neighbour. I don't know her name, she's a blow-in, moved here after I went off to Holland. I'm not in the mood for pleasantries. 'Lovely day,' she says. 'Yes a lovely day,' I say back. My second social hurdle of the day over. Only breathing and eating come natural these days. And natural makes me think of cervical swipes and hooks for rupturing membranes, so I start to walk again.

I tick off my to-do list in my head. Air out spare room bedding, iron pile of clean clothes, give toilet a lick. Still have to talk to solicitor. She expects me to go through all Mam's papers, sort out any official documents, records of bank accounts and that kind of thing. Or to organize someone else to do it. Like I give a shit right now. Like Mam's money is my business. I can't sift through her room. My mother's room is still Mam's.

10,000 miles
My own true love
10,000 miles or more

This morning I'm aiming for Mac's house. Another appointment to see the midwife today, so I'm trying my best to get this baby moving. Low clouds fill the sky and there's no wind to send away the midges. I'm a slow-moving target, the bastards are itching up my face. My mood is bad and getting worse.

Hospital, Mac's house, the baby's birth. Mam. Everything seems too far away.

Jimmy gives me a lift to the hospital in his mark-one Escort. Original owner, the car spit-polished to within an inch of its life. He brings his spaniel for the spin. She's his current life companion, his previous dog having died on the main road three years ago. This must be Spaniel Five.

I can't hear my Mam's voice, I tell Marie the midwife. Snatches of a bedtime song she used to sing keep coming back to me and going round my head, but never her singing them. Marie blames my lack of memory on the hormones. She says I'll hear my Mam's voice again after I have the baby. Apparently that's when everything will come together. I feel as though I'm only just hanging on with the one of me. I don't know how I'll manage two.

'So who's going to be your birth partner now,' she says as I hike up my top to show my belly.

I can't look at her. I haven't even thought about it yet. I keep thinking there's loads of time left to figure that one out. Maybe I could ask one of the girls. But they're chin-deep in the real world of work: paying off car loans, saving for holidays. And Andrea is still in Kerry.

I'll get through it myself. With lots of drugs to help.

She pokes and prods me before sending me off for an ultrasound. Everything looks fine, she says, and with a bit of luck the doctor will see me soon. Lucky me, another internal. I turn to the doorway, waiting to hear Mam say stop your complaining, it's your own fault you're up on that trolley.

The rocks may melt
And the seas may burn
If I should not return

I woke up this morning with a big kick to my ribs. The baby hasn't stopped since, every kick almost knocking the wind from me, forcing me to stop to catch my breath. Maybe today's the day.

I'm halfway down to the corner house before I realise how far I've walked. Well, stomped. I hooked the headphones up to my CD player, put on some Gwen Stefani and just got out of the house. The solicitor called again today. Should have told her to piss off and leave me alone. I am the executrix, she reminded me, and it is my legal responsibility to carry out the duties of this role. I need louder music.

Even though it's a cloudless day, I'm the only one on foot. The entire village speeds past me on four wheels, quick salutes all round, not slowing for a chat. Mass, they're off to mass. Which means it's Sunday. Three weeks and three days since Mam died.

I am convinced the spaniel knew Mam was going to go well before the rest of us found out. He kept sniffing around her whenever Jimmy called over, then yapping and whining at her left shin. Fucking mole. I never noticed it getting bigger.

Donal passes by me in his red Clio van. His granny is in next to him, must be late for mass. *He* definitely doesn't slow down when he sees me, not with the old lady in the van. I mean, what age is he? You'd think I had crab lice. Who needs him, anyway? I give him the finger, hope he catches it in the rear view mirror.

'Kiss me, Kate', that's all he said to get into my knickers. I didn't cop that it's the name of a musical. And a quote from *The Taming of the Shrew*. The baby gives me a good dig in the pelvis when I remember this. I haven't told him that the baby might be his. I guess he assumes the condom worked. It's my own fault. And then shagging Tony before he headed up to Dublin. What was I doing? Back living in Rosscahill with my sick mother and what did I do but sleep with two fellas in one week. I can't even remember why I fancied either of them.

I run out of steam a good way from the house and have to sit on the stone bridge for a while. The baby kicks extra hard when I try to rest. 'Yes okay,' I say out loud. I know you want to get out. I don't want to be here either. I want another body, somebody else's problems. I want my mother to get the fuck back here. I want her never to have left. I want somebody else to worry about probate and overdue babies and whether any man will want me now I'll have a child. I want to be back in college, I want the last nine months of my life back and I want my Mam back. I want to forget how my mother's naked body looked when I undressed her for a shower. How she was skeleton and skin and smooth from the chemo. I want to forget her fucking piss pot under the bed and the nights I spent beside her, waiting for her breath.

I want to be twenty-three, the way twenty-three is supposed to be.

Oh don't you see
That lonesome dove
Sitting on an ivy tree

I lie in bed listening to the dawn chorus. Something's clicked in my brain and I can hear birds louder than they can possibly sing. I turn on *Sky News* to drown them out at five this morning and still I can hear them. The cuckoo is the worst, I can pick it out above all the other birds, it echoes steadily, never changing its tune. I hate that I can hear them but not see them.

Walking under trees I feel as if the birds are bound to fall down on top of me, there are so many of them singing. How I never heard them before I'll never know. I'm walking slow today, now that the baby isn't kicking me. Not once since I ate breakfast.

That cuckoo is still calling for a mate. I can't tell where it is, where the sound is coming from. I wonder is it the same one, following me down on my walk. I have a little baby inside me. I have friends in college. I have neighbours. So why the hell do I feel so alone?

My baby. I haven't felt a kick since breakfast. My watch says it's just gone noon. 'Should I call the midwife? Or is it too early to worry?' I realise I'm saying these things out loud and that there's no one to reply. And I don't know what I'm doing.

What would Mam say? 'Follow your instincts. You'll know what to do when the time comes. I'll be here.'

Comfort words. But I still can't hear her speak them. I can sing more of her lullaby every day, my memory coming back with every step outside. I sit in her room in the morning, at night, when I can't sleep. I see Mam, see her in her velvet skirt, playing Queen Maeve before tuning in to the *Late Late Show*. I smell her perfume, her skin scent a mix of E45 lotion and peat smoke. She kept the range solid fuel, added oil-fired central heating to the house, but liked turf too much to convert the range. I don't know why I can't hear her voice.

Almost home and still no kicks. I run my hand over my belly, trying to feel life. I can still feel the baby's heel tucked just under my rib, a slight bulge in my side. It doesn't move when I rub my palm gently over it. A short poke and still no reaction.

Fuck. I can see the cherry tree now. Nearly there. I should have taken my phone with me, that's what mobiles are for. I roll my hips from side to side, trying to speed up, one hand on the side of my belly, waiting for movement inside. I hear nothing now. Every part of my being, every sense is focused on my baby, on getting this baby home. Getting this baby home safe.

My foot catches on the edge of the stone step and I tumble to the ground. My bum breaks my fall. I hold my breath, fearing I've done more damage to my baby.

A kick in the ribs makes me laugh like a crazy woman. This baby is giving out to me, I can almost feel its annoyance. No more long naps, I whisper. Not until you're out.

She's weeping for
Her own true love
As I will weep for mine

Today is a day for regrets. The clouds are grey and low in the sky, but it won't even rain. I wish it would lash rain, pour down and clean everything left out. I never told Mam how much she meant, how much I admired her. She knew I loved her, I think. God, did I even tell her that? I should have told her more. How she made the best cup of tea.

The radio filters through, even though I only left it on low for background noise. The house is too quiet, too empty since Mam left. I can't seem to fill it. Gerry Ryan on about cancer, new ways to diagnose it early using dogs. Apparently they can smell it. That explains the reaction of Jimmy's spaniel. Maybe if we'd spotted it earlier … I'm not going down that road, not even going to let myself think that one through again.

I flip the radio over to Today FM. Ray Darcy going on about the Leaving Cert. Parents and teens in a panic, as if that's what decides your life. Try a dead mother, mid-college and up the duff. That'll decide more than any state exam.

She is supposed to be here for all this shite. She is supposed to watch me fuck it up, be here when things go wrong. Give out to me when I drag my feet. Hold my little baby when I get too tired.

'Are you ready to head into the village now?' I nearly jump out of my skin when Jimmy appears outside my kitchen window.

Forty all the way to the village, then I convince him I'll be fine on my own in the supermarket. I'm fed up with the neighbourly help and attention, I want to be alone. Well, I don't tell him that, instead I say

'I'll be fine' three times. And I am, all the way down the veg aisle, past the butcher's counter. Until I reach the breakfast cereals.

Then I see Mam. She's bending down to pick up a large bag of porridge oats. Flahavan's. Her skirt hem skims the ground as she bends her knees for the extra reach. I stop at the start of the juice section. I can't move, I'm afraid she'll disappear if I do. And all I can think is, how come I can see her as plain as flowers but I can't remember her voice?

The woman moves away, chooses her porridge and goes up to pay. Mam disappears as soon as she straightens—it isn't her, just some late-forty-something picking up porridge for the breakfast. That's when the tears start and the other shoppers walk the long way around to avoid me, the fat pregnant girl spilling tears all over the juice aisle. I sense a shop assistant about to come over, concern in the air around her. I duck my head down, run for the freezer. It'll be chips for tea again.

I get Jimmy to drop me off at the corner house. I walk all the way back home, the full half mile.

Oh come back
My own true love
Stay a while with me

Almost twenty-four hours later and I'm still crying. Through a chip buttie supper, a repeat of *ER*, catnaps on Mam's bed, an early shower, and now the first steps of my walk. My crying has gone from silent dripping tears to dry heaves and back again. I'm worried the baby's getting dehydrated, with this much fluid loss. Jimmy keeps stopping by, poking his head around the door just to see if I'm all right.

'I don't need anyone,' I say. He tells me that all this crying is scaring him. But I can't stop. It's the first time I've cried since the funeral. I thought my tears were used-up back then. I'd stuffed a football-sized wad of soggy tissue into my pocket and sipped my tea, let the condolences wash over me. And I'd thought, that's it, if I cry anymore I'll shrivel up like a raisin. I guess I didn't have the energy for it anymore.

I can feel everything more intensely through the tears. The butter melting on my toast hits my nostrils so I can almost feel the smell. The house seems different. Each room has taken on its own spirit. Even the nursery—set up quickly in the spare room before Mam died— seems alive. I know I should allow myself to enjoy this new sense. But I resent it. I think life shouldn't be coming back to normal, let alone finding a new normal. I miss the numbness, I had gotten used to it.

Now the tears are slower, but steady enough to distract me from any bustling. So even out walking down the low road now, I can feel the empty space left by Mam. I can feel her absence.

She won't be coming back. I knew this already, in my head, but I couldn't feel it. It just didn't feel real. Every waddle-step down the low road brings me further away from her, from the Mam that used to live here. All that's left is an echo of her, in the way the six different potted ferns all live in the shower, the way the three-piece suite faces the range instead of the telly. Moveable things.

The singing in my head starts again, more verses, almost all of them. Still Mary Black.

I'm thinking of my baby.

For if I had a friend
All on this earth
Then you'll be a friend to me, my dear

Two days to go before they induce me. I'm booked in for nine o'clock.

Mam's Month's Mind mass is tonight. Last stage of official mourning. Now I'm expected to pick up and get on with things. Getting out for my daily waddle is an escape. Just to get out of the house. One foot in front of the other, the skin on my face still dry and stretched from crying. I think I lost a layer of skin somewhere.

Everything seems to be getting to me.

Tony rang today. He's back after his eight-month contract. Wanted to know if I'd meet up for a drink. I mean, how thick can guys get? I'm about to drop a baby. Not exactly a pop out for a drink kind of girl right now. And Donal's as bad, in his own way. Too busy with his accounting exams to bother calling over. It's as though I got up the duff and became invisible. I don't get it, how could you miss me, with the size of me? I wonder if I could convince them to take paternity tests. Just to find out. I've never let on to either of them they could be the father. But, fucksake, do the sums. They both did okay in the Leaving Cert. Donal even did Honours Maths. Maybe I'm better off on my own.

The green smell of the trees and fields brings me back to my school years, before we all left for college. The hours spent hanging around down here, heading to the corner house to escape home. And my mother.

I can barely stand up with the weight of my belly. Time to move on, see if I can evade a cervical swipe. I can almost see the corner house. I can't figure out how I've made it this far, it's so awkward to walk now. The first pain comes the moment I try to calculate how long it's going to take me to walk the half-mile home.

Shit. I hold the bottom of my belly with one hand, bend over slightly and grip the top edge of a stone wall with the other hand.

Okay, I can do this, I say to myself when the pain has passed. I can't think when the cramping starts.

That one wasn't too bad. Now, where's my phone. I start to panic when I can't find it in my jacket pockets. Not in the inside pocket either. Okay. Shit. I need to calm down. I start to sing Mam's lullaby, verse by verse, slow as I can. I make it all the way to the end before the next contraction starts.

Shit. I should have timed it.

On the next break, I find my phone in the back pocket of my maternity jeans. Midwife. Call not connecting, signal too low. Only one bar. Shit. I can't move, I'm afraid to leave the wall in case a contraction starts again. *When* a contraction starts again.

I sing the lullaby again, thinking it worked the last time. My own voice, not Mam's, not Mary Black's. Right out loud. 'As cracked as your mother,' I say in the middle of it. I lose my place, forget the next verse when I realise. That was Mam. That was just what she would say. And exactly how she would say it. Her voice.

Another cramp starts, worse than before. I squeeze the damn wall until it's over.

Then I get started. I unlock my phone and text—HELP BABY CMING B4 CORNER HSE GET ME NOW—and send it to every number in my phone.

FLOODLANDS

You would know you had been born on the wrong day when you got off the bus in Knock, County Mayo, all of seven miles from your mother's house in the townland of Farnagh. One long look up and down the main street—souvenir shops turning it into a corridor of Catholic trinkets, selling worship in a Jesus clock, a Mother Theresa garden statue, a two-foot tall plastic Blessed Virgin Mary, blue veil and all—one look and you would say, yep, that's bad luck for you.

Most of the people would use the prevailing gait. Slow. So you would always be able to spot the outsiders long before you could see their faces, their gangly walk betraying Teenager, or too much bustle saying Young Mother doing the messages with Baby left in the car.

If you walked too close to the bypass on a rainy day in August, you would picture the things you could leave behind.

*

Sometimes, to stay sane in a place where people forget how it feels to be seventeen years old on the last Saturday in August before you start your Leaving Cert year, you have to go somewhere, anywhere, so you'll stop shouting at your mother. 'These are the different types of knives I would use to chop you into pieces, these are the ways I would shut you up,' you would say if you stayed. So you meet up with Glen, or Barry, or Ciaran, or better still, all three, and you head out in the car Ciaran borrowed from his Mam, an old Toyota Starlet, the bit of sun that makes it past the clouds sparking off the bonnet so you feel like you're made, all you have to do is crank the window down, take a spin past the old labour house, see if the guy who converted it into a recording studio has any famous guests. See what else the world would bring you, other than old ladies in polyester cardigans and their fellas in Farah slacks. You park up the road, where you can see through the garden, straight into the studio window. Taking turns to guess whose shadow you could be looking at.

'Give us a go driving, Ciaran, I need to practise for my test,' you say, hoping he'll let you get behind the wheel. The last time you drove, Mam wouldn't let you take the car outside the empty car park.

Ciaran pulls over, takes the car out of gear and swops over seats with you.

'Sound,' you tell him. 'Sound.'

Into first, clutch up to the biting point, mirrors and blind spot, and you're off. In control, you head off away from town so you can get up to speed on the N17.

'And wait till you try that new game,' Glen says. 'It's mental, you can only get to the next level when you go online and win a battle against another player, there's people charging now to compete and lose for ya.' Glen is into instant messaging and gaming and anything that involves buttons, and keeps on talking tech stuff while you drive, bouncing stories across the car in random spurts, inventing lives for the people in the houses you pass.

'C'mon Alan, where are you going? Nothing to see out here,' Barry says, but you keep driving, distracted by the rush of metal.

When you've been spinning down the same road for too long and you run out of possibilities, you pull over to the side of the road right next to a homemade grotto with a statue of Our Lady. Time to practise a three-point turn. Pull it forward, turn the wheel as far as it will go, stop and take the car out of gear. No cars coming, into reverse, clutch up and accelerate and—

'Feck it's Father Martin, must be a boy scout jamboree on,' Glen jokes and your foot is too heavy because you're laughing—

Thunk.

'Fuck,' you think you say as your head jerks forward and back. The car stalls.

'What the fuck was that?' someone says but all you can think is fuck fuck fuck. It's Ciaran's Mam's car; you're not insured to drive it. Did Father Martin notice you driving? The lads will cover for you, you think. As long as no one says any different, you'll be grand. Fuck.

All four of you pile out of the car. The boot of the car is a bit dented and the bumper is cracked. The Blessed Virgin Mary hasn't gotten off so lightly though—she's been knocked off her pedestal, and her hands must have taken the hit. They're a foot away, still joined together in prayer, still wrapped in rosary beads. You stand there, looking, unsure of what to do.

'Fuck,' says Glen. 'Let's get out of here.'

Ciaran's back at the wheel, you've promised him whatever he wants if he'll cover for you. You'll get the money, somehow, honest. And he's cool, he's always been cool.

'Sound,' you say, that's it, and the four of you drive down to the village, drive up and down the main street a few times, checking out the three young ones parading past the closed-up shops, their short skirts flicking back and forth over legs stained with fake tan.

Your mind rages with what you would like to do. Sit close to one of them, feel the softness of her cheek against yours, the fine stroke of her forearm, just sit still and breathe in her calm. Or else squeeze every inch of her until you could almost claim her, how good that would feel, just to let go and follow your body as roughly as it could go. And you don't question this, don't worry whether your impulse is wrong. Your head spins with the want to do both of these things, the gentle comfort and the ride, until you wonder how the hell you'll manage to do what you're supposed to, whatever that is. Or when you will next get the chance.

A car pulls out in front of you, blocks the road. 'Right so,' Glen says, 'that's mass over.' Time to park up, head over to the bus stop, watch the holier people of Knock find their cars, see if they brought their daughters.

When you catch a glimpse of the town out of the corner of your eye, it looks as though it's peeling off, one massive bad paint job covering everything up—only close up would you see the bunch of fake flowers in the front window of Mrs Henderson's terraced house, her other front room turned into a tea room, the BVM perched on the windowsill. When you look at Knock out the window of a moving car, slowing down for the tourists in polyester slacks, Knock would look like a different character: the new bits that spring up on the edge of town shine like children.

A group of people cluster around the side of the Basilica, not far from where the miracle happened. Eejits must be waiting for Herself to show up again, or for Her statue to move or cry or something. Eejits.

Your bad luck could hang over you like a cloud, the way you would have to crash Ciaran's Mam's car the first time you'd driven it in ages, your very own moving statue, or the way nothing exciting ever happened here—one visitation back in 1879 and not one interesting thing since—or how your eyebrows never grew back after Glen waxed them off with his sister's kit the time you passed out drunk in the garden shed. And after that, the way Glen's sister looked at you, the scorn and the pity, until you wouldn't know which glance was worse.

Soggy pink bus tickets stick to the soles of your shoes, remind you of how easy it is for some people to leave the place, how they can just fire their passes off the bus, not even bother with the bin at the top of the road.

'Did ya hear Boyce got into IT?' Ciaran says this as if it is a charm, guaranteed to get you money, a girl, and wheels to bring you wherever you want to go. You talk about different colleges, who is going where, how much money they will make when they leave. Visions of Merc CLXs dance in your heads, and though none of this seems real on a Saturday evening after Mass in the Basilica, you need to think all this make-believe will add up, will come to something, that all this grind-for-hours and choose-the-right-class and stay-out-of-trouble when trouble is a label other people put on something that started out as fun, that all this *must* and *should*, will lead to something you want. Something you could have.

'I didn't think he'd make it past the Mocks,' you say.

'Yeah well, he swotted his ass off after JJ's accident.'

You look down at your feet, the four of you, studying your laces for something to say, knowing you need to fill this gap fast, before it sucks you down into itself.

'Mum says I can have her car when she gets a new one,' Barry says, and you jump on the change.

'What, you're going to drive that heap of shit? The little orange Fiat? You'll be lucky to make it as far as the main road in that box—and you can forget about pulling, you'll be lucky to get old Mrs Kelly—'

'At least everyone will see you coming,' Glen says. 'And no more waiting for Ciaran's mother to let him take the car. When's she getting rid of it?'

'January,' Barry says, and with that one word you slump down a little. One more thing to wait for, one more freedom postponed.

'Howaya, Alan,' someone says, and you look over to see little Mrs Moran standing on the path, talking at you. 'How's your Mam? Did she get on all right up in Galway? Thank God they didn't keep her in too long, no matter how good the hospital is, it isn't the same as your own home—and does she need any help around the house now?' You know better than to wait for a pause to let you answer any of the questions. 'Must be hard for you, on your own, the two of you ...' Her voice trails off, waiting for you to tell her the details of how difficult it is, how desperate your mother is for help, not so she can offer help but just so she can tell everyone she knows that Mary McGowan can not manage her own life.

'Old bag,' you feel like saying to Mrs Moran. But you don't, you just comment on the weather and ask her how her new hip is going, the way you were reared to do it. No messing, be nice to the neighbours, you never know when you might need them, mass on a Sunday until you're old enough to slink out the back with the boys, head down to the schoolyard for a smoke. A parallel universe to the one you're looking for.

You think of the things you said to your own mother, sometimes letting them out of your head, through your mouth, like the times she starts talking about your Future. 'It's too bad you weren't able to do honours Biology so you'd have another science subject to get you into Engineering. Ah well, you've only got the brains you were born with ...' And you would listen to her drift off like that, you would try to keep your words to yourself. 'Ah well, you wouldn't want to go too far from me anyway, would you. Maybe up to the Tech in Castlebar.' Just your luck you'd been born to parents who thought English was something you spoke, not a degree you could get at university. Sometimes you could go crazy with the words in your head making no sense, times like that when escape pulled as hard on you as she could push.

'Let's head,' Glen says, so you stuff your hands in your pockets and slouch up the main street. Echoes of your father's voice bounce off the walls of the buildings you pass. 'Bit of advice there, Junior. Never let a woman get cold.' A joke, getting cheap wisdom from your Dad, the first father of your class to leave, except he doesn't leave, exactly, he just moves over to the other side of Knock, sets up home with Julie and her baby, moves into her flat just beyond the shadow of the grotto.

You dawdle past the shop with ten different kinds of Knock rock on display outside—green, white and orange rock, white and blue for the Marian pilgrims, *Ireland West Airport* printed along the sugary length of one stick, the owner the same man who ran the betting shop around the back. 'Hands off, sunshine,' you could hear your Dad say. 'That's for the tourists, no child of mine's going to be seen walking down the road sucking on one of those.' And you would feel embarrassed and stupid, just because you had fancied the look of them, wondered just how sweet they would be.

'Well look who it is,' Glen says as you wander down to the roundabout. Mr Toasty dodges from exit to exit, directing the scraps of traffic that pass. He wears an old navy wool overcoat—even in high summer—and in recent years has taken to wearing big white headphones over his scraggy hair. The white lead trails behind him.

'What are you listening to?' Glen calls out. Toasty ignores him and with an elegant sweep of his arm, directs a Ford Fiesta safely towards the Basilica. You follow Glen over, don't know why, suppose it's what you always do.

'Did you not hear me? I said, WHAT ARE YOU LISTENING TO?' Glen's pushing it now.

Toasty's eyes are bright and he looks like he sees you for the first time. 'The first I learned of it was on coming from my mother's house in company with Miss Mary and at the distance of three hundred yards or so from the church. I beheld all at once standing out from the gable and rather to the west of it a figure which, on more attentive inspection, appeared to be that of the singer Michael Jackson. He stood a little distance out from the gable wall and, as well as I could judge, a foot-and-a-half or two feet from the ground.'

'Feckin madser,' Ciaran mutters.

Toaster half-turns towards a car on the road that's heading for the roundabout.

'Have you got an iPod there?' Seems as if Glen can't stop himself.

'No but I've got a fucking APPLE,' he says and pulls out a Granny

Smith, sticks the jack into it and takes a bite.

'C'mon,' you say, you just want to get away from here now. 'C'mon, leave him alone.' And you give Glen's arm a nudge then turn back on the quiet, slip Toasty the €3.75 you had in your pocket and join the other three heading back over to the village, slagging and messing on the way.

The four of you slow down outside the red-fronted shop called 'The Wild Rover' to gawp at the old hippy who runs the place, your mind flashing with the time you told Dad the rumour about the music shop. How you had heard that somebody was going to sell instruments out of the empty unit next to Keohane's. You had visions of Telecaster guitars and black Marshall amps, impromptu sessions in the back of the shop on a Saturday afternoon. 'It'll never happen, trust me,' he had said. 'A music shop in Knock, are you mad? Sure all you can play is air guitar.' Then he had laughed, shut you up more surely than if he had taped your mouth closed.

He was right, though. When the shop opened, it sold decorative bodhráns, plastic-tipped tin whistles, more tat for the tourists that were bussed out here, bad weather and good. Didn't stop him from grounding you when he found out you were with Glen when he tagged the shop's door with his signature at the time, a long O with a slash down the middle. 'A fucking cunt,' your dad laughed, 'what's he doing painting a fucking cunt all over town for?' Laughing again, laughing so hard you couldn't even start to defend your mate, all you could do was stare at your shoes, let the dark wash through you and get rid of the sense you were missing something.

Dad's voice jumping around your head, the short lines he would say to you. All the things you didn't do, or shouldn't have done. Born on the wrong day, under the wrong star, the wrong village sign.

The playground outside the national school is empty. Wind blows an empty crisp packet past your ankles to join the cigarette and roach ends that gather in the shelter of the low green wall, the paper bags, juice boxes, the can of coke with the smoky hole in the side. Glen kicks a small pink sock out of his way, swaggers over to the side entrance of the prefab. You wonder should you tell him he's got purple chewing gum stuck to the arse of his jeans.

Trouble is written all over him, he's humming with it. But then, he always has that, and the three of you know what he is like, have come to expect it. None of you say anything when Glen picks up that stone, balances it first in his right hand, then his left. You know where he is going with this, how his mind works. And you like the edge that develops around the four of you; one wrong step and you could fall off.

'Too bad I didn't bring my cans,' he says. 'This prefab could do with some colour.'

'Listen to you, you fucking poof,' Ciaran says, 'going on like your man from that show, the poof that does all that interior design crap.'

'Are you startin'? Are you? If you don't watch yourself, I'll put some colour in your fuckin' face.'

And they square up, half-messing, half-ready to have a go at each other, the unspent energy welling up inside of them, threatening to spill out.

'Yeah, well, he'll need all the hobbies he can get where he's going,' you hear yourself saying, trying to break them up and join in at the same time, wanting to be part of them. Glen raises his eyebrows at you, waiting for the punch line, waiting to get back. 'Rehab at the age of seventeen, in fairness they're probably keeping a cell for you in Mountjoy for when you turn eighteen.'

Everyone laughs, and you have them. Even Glen, delighted his myth has grown. You watch him skin up, licking the rolling papers deftly, not seeming to care that he's already been up in court. He pulls out a bottle of Ribena and a tube of Rubex, tells you he's taking all the vitamin C he can manage to help screen the hash in the drug tests.

You tune out the sound of Glen planning the destruction of the prefab window by window; fix on the harvest flies gathering on the sunny side of the building. Let the hash settle into you, bring you back into yourself. Picturing your mother, at home at the ironing board, looking for one more thing she can straighten out, your father driving the twenty-five miles over to the toy shop with his adopted daughter in the booster seat, him and his fiancée indulging this plump saint. Thinking about the lies your parents told you, how now you know that there is nothing you can do, you were out of luck before you were even born. When it comes down to it, people lie, tell you what they think matters, what they want you to believe—Santa Claus, the tooth fairy, a vengeful God. Whatever suits them, gives them something over you.

It looks like Glen is ready to start; you watch him toss the rock from hand to hand. Take a lungful, feel indifference settle into your bloodstream. A laugh bubbles up when the rock Glen throws rebounds right back off the first window, but you hold that laugh in, holding the energy that comes up with it, keeping it for yourself. Another pitch, overhand and harder this time, and another bounce. You saunter over to the window, examine it for marks. 'Maybe it's bullet-proof,' you say to Glen, picking with your little finger at the small chip left by the rock.

'Maybe you're too much of a poof,' Ciaran says, winding it up again.

Another lungful and you back off from the window, over to the edge of the playground, letting the distance between you show. The hash thickens the air around you so you can almost see how separate you are, as if this scene is a game you're playing on your Xbox, all the action on a screen.

A few minutes more of Glen and his game and you go off on your own. You stop, look back once when you hear your name. But they've got their backs to you, they're watching Glen try to get that stone through the window, and looking for bigger stones. So you drift down the main street, past the useless shops, past the grotto and the pilgrims. All the way down to the end of the strip because you don't want to stay in a national school playground on a Saturday evening in the third week of August, watching Glen Walsh try to get a stone through the last window of the school prefab. You walk past Tara, her arm around the waist of some blonde-haired fella, and you remember how small her hands were, how you thought you might have something there, back before her brother JJ kicked it in the crash.

'Hey Alan.'

'Hey Tara.' You don't want to have to stop.

'Were you down at the Basilica?'

Sigh. Now you have to stop. 'Nah. Why?'

'Didn't you hear? Michael Jackson stopped by on his way to the airport. Turns out he was doing some recording over at the old workhouse.'

'Come off it, you're taking the piss.' She had to be taking the piss. No way Toasty could have been in his right mind.

'Nah, I seen him myself. He signed a few autographs, you know, he was really cool. I think he wanted to see where Our Lady appeared.'

'Fucksake.' Crappy luck all around. Something finally happens in this hole and you walk right past it.

Tara looks wicked hot. You try not to wish it was your waist she was holding, how that would feel; you just move on, say nothing. And when you get to the bus stop you keep walking in the direction of home because you are in no hurry to hear your mother say, 'Will you clean out the grate and will you think about what you're going to do after the Leaving' again, figure you will take the scenic route over the hill, along the river, cut the seven miles of road down to five, hike up past the daisies that cluster on the top of the dry bank, swaying in the mild breeze, where you can run your open palm along the tops of them, the hash intensifying the touch, the light tickle, glad no one else would see you. You walk home because you have nowhere else to go, but you walk slow, wishing that you had a brother or sister waiting there, so you wouldn't be the only one.

You would think about Glen, and your Dad, JJ's accident, how soft that girl's skin looked, all the possibilities spread out after the

Leaving, after your eighteenth year, walking along the grassy bank of the narrow river, dug out of the ground a hundred years ago to let the water drain out of the land, to stem the floods that threatened every year.

You would think about all these things if you weren't so busy trying to figure out where to go and how you would get out, as you ambled between the stream and the bus route, beneath the flight path. Walking along the three ways to slip away.

EXILE 88

Brian finds it odd, hearing Maura rush around getting ready for work. That she has work-clothes again, after twenty-odd years. He stays out of her way, skulks around the living room with the curtains closed, a pair of tracksuit bottoms pulled over his y-fronts. Tries to get the sound of The Bangles out of his head. *Today's best music, today.* Only one more night on the couch, then back over to London. One more night exiled to the living room.

The girls rattle around the kitchen after their mother has managed to drag them out of bed. Ailish's voice carries into the living room, but Clare's is too quiet, as ever. He hears the words 'last night', and curiosity drags him into the kitchen to make a cup of tea he doesn't want. Ailish stops talking when he walks in, but his older daughter is more subtle. Clare slips into school banter, giving out about how much homework she's getting in fifth year. Neutral territory. Brian keeps an eye on her, notices she puts a spoon of salt into her tea instead of sugar.

'I'll leave you to it so,' he says to them, wondering what they were up to last night when they were supposed to be at their friend's house.

One thing is certain—he'll only find out as much as they want him to know. He folds the blanket, puts it on top of the pillow at the end of the couch. He's the outsider here.

RTE Radio One blasts from the radio on top of the fridge as Brian cleans up the mess in the kitchen. Maura's gone to work and the girls are at school, then hockey.

He drops the Pyrex casserole dish while drying it with the right towel—not the one Maura set out for hands—and shouting back at *Liveline's* ignorant caller. At least the dish broke in two large chunks, only a few splinters off the edge where it hit the lino. A quick sweep and they're gone. He holds the two halves of the dish, one in each hand, looking around, worried. This isn't his house anymore. He doesn't want Maura to get angry with him—she's resentful enough, simmering beneath every word.

The two pieces fit together, just well enough to look whole.

'That'll do,' he says. It takes a few doors before he finds the cupboard where the cookware lives. The casserole dish fits behind the stack of disposable pie plates and mismatched bowls, and he slots the two pieces in so the broken edges join together. He raises his eyebrows, inspects. Looks fine, you'd never know.

The house is his for another few hours. He wanders through the rooms when he should be sorting through boxes pulled down from the attic. Childhood relics, mostly—posed black and white photos, a statue of Our Lady that had belonged to Maura's mother, funeral cards, an old letter from his uncle in India—his and Maura's lives mingling in the one box. Then things from when the girls were younger—worn stuffed animals and crayon pictures—that at the time they couldn't bear to give away. He's tempted to dump it all, say nothing, but he figures he's done enough damage already.

Ailish and Clare's rooms are off-limits, shrines to teenage

obsessions. Maura's bedroom is off-limits too. The bedroom they used to share. All his clothes are already back in London, he'd brought them over shirt by shirt throughout the last decade. Even the good suit.

In the living room, he picks through the stack of records. Early Beatles, a best of Joe Dolan, Nana Mouskouri. Brian pulls out the Elvis 78s. He can't remember who bought them, but they must be worth something. Plus, he was the real Elvis fan. Maura preferred listening to John Denver.

Elvis goes into the box in the middle of the room, with everything else he has filtered out of his past life. Old work references, his college certificates, photos from Seapoint Ballroom back in the sixties, him and his friends looking optimistic.

He puts Don McLean's 'Vincent' on the turntable. 1972. It reminds him of the morning he walked into the ward after Clare was born: Maura, asleep in bed, the ends of her short hair sticking to her face, a little bundle curled up next to her. The ward sister told him Maura wouldn't let them take her baby away to the nursery. His wife looked beautiful, vulnerable, fierce. When she woke up, her face glowed, and she pulled him close, introduced him to their new baby. That was the moment he felt most in love.

He had been lucky to get work in London. Sometimes the fact that he was born there went in his favour. The Irish connections helped too. God knows there isn't work for a surveyor here in Galway. Or anywhere else in Ireland for that matter. They'd been lucky he could support the family—two young daughters able to grow up in the same town he and Maura had been raised in.

The few visits home every year used to be the best holidays; he'd bring the car over on the boat and they'd go off on trips, the four of them. And the whispered phone calls to Maura used to be so sexy.

Now he wonders was it really all that great, or if London put a veneer on it.

He steps softly into her bedroom. 'Our bedroom,' he says. It was never this tidy when they shared it—there isn't one pair of dirty socks on the floor, not a shirt or vest flung over the chair. The blanket is pulled right up over the pillows, tucked in like a hotel bed. A row of bottles and a small wooden box sit on the dresser. Perfume, a jar of cotton balls, something called Astral All Over Moisturiser.

There is a basket in the corner of the bedroom, and he lifts the lid. In the bottom of it he sees a small bundle of underwear. Silky, not like the practical cotton ones she used to wear.

He pulls out the narrow top drawer, touches the baubles she has kept. A smooth polished piece of amber catches his eye, clear but for the fly trapped in it. He holds it in his palm, keeps it there. Figures why not, she'll never notice.

The phone rings, startles him out of the bedroom. It's Maura, to say she won't be home until after six, she has a few messages to do. He knows she's avoiding him, staying out for any cock-and-bull excuse.

The girls get home first. Almost everything is where it should be.

'Hi Dad, what did you do, throw all the dirty dishes out?' Ailish, always the joker. Clare keeps her thoughts to herself but offers her dad an apple when she gets one. He takes it, even though he doesn't like them.

It's ten years since he lived here full-time. No point explaining that he's trying to be helpful. This morning he remembered to open the living room curtains, fold the blanket and sheet. In London, the housekeeper takes care of these things. Maura used to rage at him for how messy he was—newspapers on the bathroom floor, cups left anywhere—things his housekeeper won't let him away with anymore.

Maura gets home early, after all. 'Did you get much done today?'

He pictures the Pyrex dish as she moves around the kitchen, pulling out pots and pans and vegetables. 'Do you want me to cook for a change?' A question for a question.

She looks at him as though he's grown an extra head. 'Since when did you start to cook?'

Except it's not a real question. He knows better than to take the bait, so he answers the first one, keeps an eye on the corner cupboard. 'Got most of it sorted. Just the shed and a few bits and bobs left to do.' Give her what she wants. The last thing he needs is a row.

'What's the story with Clare?' The question pops out before he has a chance to think about it. The girls are upstairs doing homework and it's been tugging at him all day.

'What do you mean?'

'I caught her putting salt into her tea this morning. Are you sure she was out at the friend's house at all last night?'

Maura's face shuts right down. 'Are you saying something? That I'm not keeping track of my teenage daughters, Mr Over-on-holidays-from-London?'

He takes a long breath through his nostrils. 'Just wondering if she's drinking. That's all.'

'She's alright,' Maura says. 'It's the other one I'm worried about. Ailish is the one spending time with the boys, thinks I don't know. Flirts like her father.'

He doesn't know where to go after this, so he tries for concern. 'What about you, are you alright?' He knows she's pissed off working in a shop. She had to give up nursing when they got married; the nuns wouldn't keep her on once she had a man to look after her.

Maura is on him like a flash. 'Don't you go thinking that I don't want this too. You should see the face I've had to put on everyday for my family, the neighbours, at mass when I used to go. "Brian's great, doing really well. Yes, I'm so lucky to have him, working so hard for us over in London." And then I ring you and you barely talk.'

Brian doesn't say much after that. How can women just spew this stuff out, when all he said was are you okay? Why dig up the past? He finds he has a lot of questions recently, and not a lot of answers.

Out in the shed, he picks through flowerpots and leftover roof-tiles. Some of his tools are still in good nick; he sorts them into a plastic crate, decides to leave them behind, in case Maura ever needs to cut a piece of wood or level out a shelf.

Only the attic boxes in the living room are left, then he's done. Maura has already sifted through the junk room. She gave away his old Subbuteo set, and left the box of match programs out for him. Paperwork and family photos had been sorted long ago, any happy wedding images wiped away.

Just one more night to go.

The next morning, he's the first up for breakfast. He checks on the Pyrex dish. Relief. It hasn't been touched; no one has mentioned it. A memory surfaces: the time Ailish broke the frog mirror, placed the shards back into their frame and put it back up on the bathroom windowsill as if nothing had happened. He's amazed to think about the big deal he made of it at the time, giving out stink to her, and she must have been only six or seven. She was lucky she didn't get cut, but then, wasn't everyone?

Brian is starting to feel as if he is no longer here by the time he's got the car loaded up and goes back in to say goodbye.

Ailish is teary; Clare sits at the kitchen table, flipping through a teen magazine, moody and disinterested. His wife—ex-wife—is checking the rooms for anything he might have left behind, awkward and hurrying him. As always.

'Off you go,' she says. Not *safe home*.

When he steps through the front door, Brian wonders will he be like a photograph, a memory kept in the bottom of a box up in the attic, left there just in case.

The girls have drifted down the hallway to hover behind their mother.

'Bye,' he says.

He wishes he had more for them. He pictures the Pyrex dish, the two halves cradled in the kitchen cupboard. 'And watch out for sharp edges.'

MONOLOGUES

PREP

The nurse avoids me, skirting my crossed legs, skimming past my eyes, focusing all her attention on my mother as she helps her turn over onto her side so she's facing me, shows her how to pull her knees all the way up so she's in the foetal position. My mother looks at me with a blank face, free of make-up, expressionless.

'Please stay,' she says. I don't want to stay.

And I wonder if I'm imagining the uncertainty behind her pupils, the possibility of fear. I'm not even sure she has said these words out loud.

The ward smells of bodily functions, the indignity of blood and excrement and urine and sweat mixing with the oxygen, made public. Here in the small room where my mother's spine will be tapped, the scent follows me, clinging to my clothes and the inside of my nose. This stench battles with another, more acrid smell, what I hope is antiseptic, but which seems more like singed feathers.

Nurse—for this is how I have come to think of this petite woman, as if her name and job are one and the same—hikes up the back of my mother's tunic, lays a surgical sheet across her exposed bottom. She rubs some gel onto the small of her back, disinfectant by the smell of it, and my mother's eyes almost close. She's enjoying the attention, I think. All that touchy-feely fussing. *Are you okay, Mrs Morris, can I get you anything, would you like another blanket Mrs Morris?* Lording it and milking it.

'Remember how Mamó used to pull down her stockings when her legs got too hot,' my mother says, 'right down to her ankles, do you remember?'

'Mm-nh,' I say, knowing what's coming next, having heard this story over and over since I could understand words, if not the meaning behind them. She's up to her old tricks, pretending she's invulnerable, talking herself into a stronger place. I wish I could open a window, get some of the petrol fumes from the car park up here into this small room with a bed dropped in the middle. Anything to drown out the hospital smell.

'And then there was the time she did it in front of the priest, next door at Sarah's house, oh heavens above! It was unreal. She started to sweat and she pushed down the two knee-highs, the pair of them, all the way down around her ankles, there she was sitting on a kitchen chair talking away to the priest—Father Michael wasn't it, no, Father Dominic was there by then—and up she gets to help Sarah in the kitchen with the tea, and doesn't the dog get back in somehow, they always kept their dogs indoors, a disgrace—'

'If you would just move your left leg up a little Mrs Morris,' Nurse says when my mother pauses to take a breath. She pulls her leg closer to her chest and holds onto it.

'—her best stockings flapping around her ankles as she walks, then doesn't the dog make a run for them, grabs the top of one of her stockings and pulls hard, so hard he pulls the legs right out from under her and doesn't she go flying, legs out like that—' and she spreads her knees apart, the surgical sheet lifting like a tent '—and the old priest gets a full view of her knickers! Then she says—after pulling her skirt back down—then she says "Father, If I'd known I'd be showing you my knickers today, I'd have worn a better pair!" Just like that!'

She's laughing so hard as she's telling it, the hospital sheet is starting to slip off with each successive body shake. I just raise my eyebrows and nod, let out a 'hunh' so she knows I'm listening. Sort of.

Nurse leaves the room, taking the indulgent atmosphere with her. But not before warning my mother that the doctor will be around in a few minutes. As though she is going to get up and wander off somewhere. Although, you never know.

On the far side of the room one of the fluorescent lights is flickering.

'Isn't that gas,' she says, 'showing the priest her knickers and not a bother on her.'

'I'd say he was fairly traumatised,' I say to her, getting back to our old script, years of listening to family tales. It doesn't matter that it's been nearly fifteen years since I left home for college and tried to find somewhere in the world I could do some good. That was what I'd thought I'd be doing when I joined Concern. Funny how helping others fades into the background and daily routine takes over. You know, checking you've brought out enough tampons, finding out where the local safe spots are, making sure you've got clean water for the day.

My mother's laugh turns to a wheeze as she tries to catch her breath. 'And Sarah trying to keep everything respectable for the priest, shutting the dogs out and everything. She nearly killed Mammy for that.'

I tried to remember the last time I heard her call my grandmother 'Mammy'. They (my mother and aunts and uncles, eight in all) always referred to her as 'Mamó', ever since her first grandchild started to talk. As though she was no longer their mother.

'Oh when I think of herself and Sarah. Always battling over

something. Going to mass, cleaning out the well. Even chicken-plucking.' Her gaze shifts behind me, and I turn towards the door, spot the doctor come in, moving in the centre of busyness, the cluster of nurses and trainee doctors adapting to every movement with minimal direction.

'All ready for you doctor,' says Nurse, as another nurse sets up a tray of instruments. The two student doctors step back from my mother's bare flesh, the vast stretch-marked reality of her.

NUMB

My mother and I never held conversations, that back and forth volley of 'how was school'—'it was fine except for the crocodile'— 'what crocodile' sort of thing. My mother preferred monologues. So even though she would start out conventionally enough with a 'good day at school', she would take my reply and find the finest thread to spin out whatever tale had been resting in her head. One day I even told her that my teacher, Mr O'Neill, had come to school dressed up as a woman—mini-skirt, tights and all—just to see how she would use it. 'London,' she had said, 'the time I had the job in a dress shop, we used to borrow the new mini-dresses to go dancing, tuck the tags in so you couldn't see them. We'd leave them back on the rack the next day, say nothing. The fellas used to be mad for us.' And off she went, in twists and twirls of platforms and going for dates on the tube and the way a man could put his hand on the small of her back.

I have heard these stories over and over since she woke up to find me in the bassinet next to her, told each time as if each repetition were a revelation; collected and (I realised as I grew up) embellished memories for the most part, some even handed down to her from her mother. She hoards stories and memories. Once she repeated back to me a bad dream I had told her about, as if it was new, and hers. I don't talk to her about my time in Mozambique. I've learned to be careful around her, to mind my words.

The doctor, or one of the nurses, drops something back on the steel tray next to my mother. Now comes the tricky part. The procedure, they call it.

Some of her stories have come to seem like my own memories, pictures conjured up and patched together from old black and white photos, little squares that have lost their borders, started to move and talk so it seems they belong to me. With some stories, it gets so I don't even hear my mother speak the words; the images flare up in my mind, the scenes imprinted there from years of telling. I can feel my last decade-and-a-half of independence start to slip away. I'm getting fuzzy again, having a hard time picturing who I am.

The doctor pulls the extendable light closer to my mother's back, and I look away. Linoleum floor, floral curtains pushed back from the bed, pastel walls, no window and too many medical supplies lined up along the walls. I focus on the pictures behind my eyes.

My mother walks along a narrow dirt road, the third Bohan to wear this particular pair of shoes. The hole in the side of them has yet to become visible enough to warrant repair, and the soles are in reasonable condition. It's Saturday afternoon and she has just dropped up a few eggs to May James' house for the baby. Each of her siblings has their own responsibilities. Jobs, my mother would call them, making them sound small, and sensible. As she is the eldest, my mother—at eleven years of age—is expected to help Mamó with the important work, the things her father can't be trusted with—baking, drawing water from the well, collecting the turf, killing the chicken for Sunday dinner.

Mamó picked her for this job as soon as she was eight or nine, old enough to start learning the outside work, and she used to set her a hen to catch after school, made it into a game. The trick was to be prepared, make sure the hen was distracted enough, then move fast and keep a good grip. My mother had the knack, after a good six months of listening to Mamó's howls, sleeves rolled up to her elbows, hands on hips as she laughed at her eldest daughter's attempts to catch a chicken.

'You'll just feel a little sting now when the needle goes in,' the doctor says, and the other medical types lean in closer, bringing the smell of antiseptic with them.

My mother always likes to tell this story; whether she means it as a warning or as a testament to her own ability to do whatever it takes to survive, I have yet to figure out. But who knows—maybe in a childhood without television, these were the images that stayed with her, the highlights.

She brings out a handful of bread crusts, just enough to get the hens to gather around her. The younger ones come pecking first, before being shoved out of the way by the three-season experts. It's one of these she's after. The pure brown one pecks at her bare toes, and that's her mind made up: he'll do for dinner. She slips one hand underneath the bird to grab its legs, and with the other hand she holds its back; one smooth motion and she's got the chicken upside down, dangling from her strong hands. Then a sharp pull up on the chicken's neck, so she feels the snap, and the wings start to flap.

In the small hospital room with the bed in the middle, my mother tries to hide a wince. The doctor doesn't notice, doesn't say a thing.

Whenever Mamó killed a chicken, she would go off and finish some other job while the bird's body went through its last convulsions, wings flapping and legs scrambling. But my mother liked to sit and watch. She felt she owed it to the chicken. (How like my mother, to sympathise with something she had just killed.) Then she would slit the throat carefully, letting the blood drain out into a bucket, and hang the bird up for plucking. She considered plucking a personal challenge and she would time herself against the number of stanzas of 'Noreen Bán' she would get through before the last feathers were pulled, ignoring the shouts from her younger brothers and sisters to shut up, knowing there wasn't much they could do to stop her. Plus she liked the rhythm, the careful tear of quill from skin, quill from skin.

Depending on her mood, my mother would end the verbal lesson in 'how to wring a chicken's neck' with the story of the time she went to three rounds of 'Noreen Bán' while she waited for the hen's body to finish dying until Mamó came out, found her singing away and the chicken still twitching, half-dead. She sent my mother into the back kitchen for the biggest knife and made her pick up that half-dead chicken, place it across a block of wood and chop its head off. 'Next time do a right job of it' was what Mamó had said to her, something I have heard my mother say often enough to me.

This is how my mother keeps herself together while the doctor injects anaesthetic into her bare lower back. These are the words she uses, conjuring Mamó with long-replayed tales, patchwork memories to blanket her.

The doctor mumbles something and goes back to his equipment.

'Next time do a right job of it,' she says to him.

PUNCTURE

She is holding my hand, and I am trying not to let her see how much I want to let go. Her grip makes me feel more uncomfortable than I already am, forcing me to be too aware of what she is going through—the tight squeezes when the needle pierces her half-deadened skin, and again when they manoeuvre the thin tube that will drain fluid from her spine. Perspiration forms between our joined skin. So much for my theories of mothers and daughters and how there should be at least two countries between us. NGO work suited me—all that time spent in countries with feeble communications set-ups. I'd take assignments abroad so fast I left vapour trails behind me.

The room is quiet, except for the sound of metal instruments as they hit the metal tray, and the odd comment from the doctor. 'Going to be a bit tricky, all this fatty tissue.'

My body is letting me down, too, in small ways. There's a rash on the knuckles of my left hand that won't fully go away, no matter what ointments I spread on them. Red patches flare up whenever I'm too hot, or if I start to think of the way I left Mozambique. The itch is turning into background noise, always there.

I wonder if I should check with the doctor that it's okay for me to stay, but I don't want to talk to him, so I focus instead on the exit interview I have re-scheduled for Wednesday.

'I had to come back, you see, it's my mother ... That's why I had to leave my job with the aid agency at such short notice ...' Lies, but I practice them to distract myself. In my head, I conjure up an interview panel sitting across the table from me: two men and a woman with rimless glasses. I don't know why, but I imagine that she's the one who does all the talking. She's the one to watch out for.

'And how is your mother now?'

Easy.

'What do you see yourself doing now that you seem to be back here in Ireland for an indefinite length of time?'

Hmmm.

'Where do you see yourself headed? Say, in five years time?

Don't roll your eyes in an interview, they never like that, even when you're planning on leaving. Resist the temptation to tell her you plan to win the Lotto and retrain as a dominatrix. Do the lovely girl act; pretend to be the woman you've tried to be for God knows how long. Stick to a sincere tone of voice, just the right balance of fake confidence and obsequiousness, so they won't question me too much. So whoever is conducting the exit interview will think 'oh what a nice girl' and won't move past that first reaction. I hope that my ears and mouth will not fail me on the spot that the real world stands. After all, what is the worst question the panel could ask me?

'Hold still now. Just another few seconds,' the doctor tells my mother.

Possibilities swish through my mind while I hold my mother's hand, absorbing her nervous sweat, waiting for the focus on her back to shift. My foot knocks against one of the wheels on the bed, and I curse. The worst question: 'Why did you leave the project halfway through?' No. Maybe: 'Why did you leave your cat behind outside your flat?' Or: 'Why didn't you give him to someone or have him put down?' Or even: 'Why did you leave them all without so much as a proper goodbye or an explanation?'

Always running off at the last minute. Never finishing a thing, trails of what could have been floating along behind me. If onlys and maybes. I picture my mistakes curled up like a foetus in a display jar: Charlie and his lines about trust, Icarus the mangy cat left to fend for himself, Marguerite and Josie trying to patch up the Women's Capital Scheme, the Mozambique women themselves (always building, working, carrying), their children. Me and my magic beans.

The doctor pats my mother's hip gently. 'Lovely,' he says. 'Got all we need.'

My mother is holding her raised knees with one hand, her other hand still grasping mine.

As the doctor drifts away, out of my immediate view, Nurse says to my mother, 'Right. Don't move now, I'll need you to stay like this for another wee while.'

She lifts her hand from mine, adjusts the front of the sheet and wraps both hands around her knees while Nurse smears more antiseptic on her lower back with small lumps of cotton wool, and fixes a square hospital bandage to the wound.

'Back in a little while to check on you,' she says in that friendly busy nurse way, already heading for the door.

And we're on our own, my mother's back still bare, the sheet draped low around her hips.

RECOVER

The rows of equipment, boxes and tubing, the stark functionality of everything in the room weighs in on me, so the walls start to seem closer and closer, my mother's presence swelling Alice-style.

'... and you know, the heating. Well I'm not sure how long ...' her voice drifts off, back the same way it drifted into my headspace. I know I should be listening.

Words, words and more words. How much can one woman have to say? How long before she runs out of words?

'... the thing is, Fionnuala,' and she leans out of the bed to grab hold of my arm, 'the thing is I want to sort out what to do with Shamie—'

'Who?'

'You know, Shamie, my pony. He's back in Killanin, in Mark's field, and I want to sort things out so he's taken care of.'

She takes her hand off me, folds her arms over in a *well now, that's that* kind of way.

'Oh for God's sake Mother,' I say, reverting to Mother now I'm pissed off with her, fed up of all this need, the pit she has dug for herself in the antiseptic comfort of a hospital day bed. 'You're going straight home once the nurse checks up on you, gives you the go-ahead. It's just a test.' I lower my voice, aim for a comforting tone. 'You'll be fine once you're back in your own place.'

My mother's eyes lock on the back of my skull, as if she can see right through my head. She looks as if she's going to give me one of those clips across the top of the head, the way she used to when I was nine. 'Yes, I most certainly will be fine, I am already doing just fine— and if you must go, if you have other things you need to be doing, well then just go.'

I don't move a muscle. I can't, not with that feral cat stare.

'Well?' she says, and it's the way she lifts her eyebrows, not another muscle in her body moving—that's it.

'No, I'm here to help you and I will stay until it's time to bring you home. I said I would drive you, so that's that,' I say. The fluorescent light is still flickering.

'Oh no, that's fine, I can get a taxi.'

'Okay then. Fine. Get a taxi.' Call her bluff. I play this game well, it's an old one. I'm going nowhere, though, slumped in my chair like a surly teenager. I realise that this is the first time I've been comfortable with my mother since I came back home.

'But maybe you should call over later, maybe stay the night.'

'What?'

'Just so you're not on your own the whole time, in that hostel place. You really should just stay with me.'

Last week she told me there probably wouldn't be enough room for me in the old cottage, and now she's telling me I should stay there for my own good. Imagine cool wet grass, hot coals, think of anything to stop myself from calling her a manipulative old cow to her face. Picture my own life. Icarus on the day I first found him: an orange kitten that scraped anyone who tried to pet him. Or the day I left, the sight of him walking in the front door, his left ear torn from his latest fight, heading straight for his food dish and ignoring me for the last time. Not much left of my own life, really. Unemployed. Single. Catless. Motionless.

'Besides,' she says, 'the nurse said I shouldn't be left on my own for the next twenty-four hours, just to be sure ...'

Guilt is layering itself on top of me, smothering my anger. 'Be sure of what?' I ask, but leave it at that. I don't want to go to the trouble of finding out if this is fabrication or not, figuring one night won't kill me. Be a better person, I tell myself, a pep talk to override my natural instinct for flight. Keep your mouth shut. *Bí i do thost*, as Múinteoir Mary used to say in second class. She is your mother after all, gave birth to you, put up with your raging hormones and only kicked you out of the house once.

'You know,' she says, leaving the unspoken argument suspended between us like a bridge, a delicate yet steel-fierce construct that connects us, 'your grandmother's favourite thing in the world was always running fast—doing anything fast, really. She always had the fastest ponies, she ran all the way down to the well and back, buckets and everything. Oh, if she had ever owned a car she would have been dangerous. She loved speed.'

We're both quiet, silence settling around us. Surface tension, that's what we suffer from—a thin skin over our relationship that we're both afraid to break. So we sit there, ignoring each other until my mother can no longer hold the silence.

'Mamó always liked her freedom, too.'

I nod, keep my words to myself, hold my space.

Each one of us assuming we know how this will play out, actions mapped in advance, as rehearsed as wringing the chicken's neck on a Saturday afternoon, as necessary.

DEEDEE AND THE SORROWS

At the back of the pub, the door is not a door it's a curtain, a heavy black one that makes Deirdre think of grand hotels and magic shows. Stephen (her manager/ex-boyfriend) pulls it aside and she follows him into the venue. Small tables look as though they could be pulled over to one side of the room to clear a space for dancing. But they're bolted down, with spindly chairs and wooden stools clustered around them. The room is cold.

What was she thinking, going on the road around Ireland in mid-November? It had seemed like a good idea back in front of a gas fire in Dublin. Just get to work, don't think about it. Set up and sound-check.

Deirdre's pink fleece pyjama bottoms snag on the end of a guitar stand and she nearly topples the entire pile. Three hours trapped in a van with five guys and she's about ready to kick someone. Owen tries to yank down her bottoms. She tells him to eff off out to the van with the other guys and help bring in the gear while she hunts down the house sound engineer. Owen's thirty, only four years younger than her, but sometimes she feels as though the age gap turns her into a handy version of his mother. One more prank like that and she might not be able to have sex with him anymore.

There's no sign of the sound guy, so she digs her phone out of her bag. Lily should be getting into bed soon. She misses her daughter; though less now that she's at the venue, now that she has had some time to recover the scattered bits of herself, glue her idea of who she is back together without the umbilical pull of Lily's four-year-old stream of questions.

'Mama, where does money come from? Who makes it? Why do you need it?' And on she goes. Deirdre mock-whispers goodnight, two kisses into the phone and then two more, asks her to put her dad back on the phone, she wants to talk to him.

'Bout what?' Lily asks.

'Stuff,' Deirdre says, not in the mood for more long-winded explanations that will only lead to more questions. 'Just give him the phone, sweetie.' She can hear Pete in the background saying something similar, and she misses Lily even less. 'Did you give her both inhalers?'

'Yep.'

'And her tonic?'

'Yes.' His voice gets tense over this one syllable, but Deirdre can't help herself.

'Don't forget she needs to have a poo before bedtime or else she'll be up at 4am with a pain in her belly.'

This time he doesn't try to hide the sigh. 'We'll be fine, stop fussing. Besides, my mum's here to help me out.'

Deirdre wishes him good luck, and disconnects. Thank God he wants to help raise Lily. And that they broke up early on. He doesn't question her itchy feet: she's lucky she can take five days and head out on the road, feel the tug of a Lily-shaped gap inside of her.

She pulls out the set list, a fresh sheet of paper from her notebook and a black marker. Day One. Galway on a Tuesday night. In a recession. Still, it's supposed to be a party town and the manager claims this is a student pub on weekdays. Move the cover of 'Girls Just

Wanna Have Fun' from her encore set to the top. 'Fishbowl' and her other songs can wait till three songs in when she is warmed up, and the crowd is warmed up.

Deirdre walks around the room, tries to get a feel for the place, pretends to help the boys as they load in the gear and scatter it in front of the low stage. Pacing calms her down, gets her ready for the gig. The house lights are up and she can see too much: the beer stains on the tabletops, the bits of silver gaffe tape left on the walls long after whatever decorations they'd once held up are gone, blobs of chewing gum and other things worn into the black wooden floor. Venues without punters are gloomy places.

A clang startles her; the stage is filling up with cases of different sizes and shapes, holding drums, guitars, keyboards. Owen steps onto the stage, hoists her handbag over his head. 'Where do you want this monster?'

It's the bag that can fit everything: a spare T-shirt, her scrapbook of random magazine clippings, an original Sony Walkman, the kind that takes cassettes. Deirdre doesn't have an MP3 player—she's the only musician she knows who doesn't—but she has an extensive back catalogue in her head and a good cassette collection. She likes the hiss of tape, the ghost-prints of other songs on tapes that haven't been played for years.

'Lob it over to me,' she says, but Owen knows better and reaches down to hand it to her. There are too many distractions up by the stage. She avoids Van's outstretched legs—he's grabbing some shut-eye to recover after the crappy drive from Monaghan—and aims for the back of the venue, figuring she can hide out behind the sound desk, get some space.

Back when the lovely girls were learning to write thank-you notes and to make suitable conversation, Deirdre chased love and the unexpected. The nuns warned her that she would end up living a life of sin, that she would end up a single mother without a penny to her name or a steady job, and on the whole, they were right.

She spots a poster for tonight's gig next to the black curtain. *Tuesday Night Special: DeeDee and The Sorrows, 9pm till late, No Support.* So she's one of the Tuesday Night Specials. Sounds like a dodgy tribute band.

Deirdre tries out the first verse of 'Fishbowl', slowly, to make sure her voice is still working. Way back when she was in school, the nuns used to stick her at the very edge of the choir, towards the back, claiming her voice would put off the rest of the girls. One nun in particular—Sister Alphonsus, a square-shaped hag—used to make her stand beside the piano and practise the songs on her own, telling the other girls that they were to listen quietly and make sure that they never sang like Deirdre. Her range is good, but she sounds raspy, though she doesn't smoke.

'Well howya, now there's a voice I haven't heard in years,' booms a voice she had finally stripped out of her head.

She turns around, face tense, shoulders tense in her old T-shirt, and sure enough, it's Liam Rynne. Last time she'd heard, he was in the Canaries, playing pub covers.

'Liam,' she says and nods. Six years. Keep it cool. He broke up with her after three intense years together, dumped her by text message on the first mobile phone she had ever owned. It took a fling with Sunbear's bass player and an unplanned pregnancy to get over him. Plus six months of writing nasty (but mostly true) things about him in black permanent marker in the toilets of any pub she went to.

'Deirdre, gorgeous,' he says and walks right by her, pats her on the shoulder on his way over to the sound desk. 'Sorry I'm late, had to run out for a spare lead.' He holds up an Ethernet cable. Still a lazy tech nerd: surfing emergency.

Great timing. She looks down at her fuzzy pyjama bottoms. Forget clean underwear in case you get into an accident, you should always wear your best jeans when travelling in case you run into the man who stole pieces of you. It's way too late for her to change bottoms— it's time for the sound check with her band of borrowed musicians:

friends who have agreed to come on the road for a five day world tour of Ireland for peanuts, who have left their girlfriends and wives and crap jobs and bands to play backup to promote her first ever solo CD. On her own independent label, IndoBabe. The album that took four Lily years to make, between nappy changes and feeding times and part-time temp jobs and too many romantic mishaps.

He's just one man, that's all, just one man. Breathe in and out and forget he's in the room.

She can easily think of at least three bad choices in her recent past—not bad men, Liam is the only one of those she has risked—but men who expected that deep down she is like the other women they know: itching to take their lives in hand, fill up the gaps that emerged once they left home. Imagining she'd be domesticated.

Forget him. Forget them all. Deirdre takes a deep breath and stands up on stage in front of the mic. Slings her bass strap over her shoulder. Waits while the guys tune and twang and plug in the bits that need plugging. Liam signals her to test the mic.

'One-two. One-two.' Eff you, eff you. She sings the first verse of 'Your Cheatin Heart', hopes the message will get through to him. Sticks her chin out.

The band is as ready as they are ever going to be, but Deirdre wants to try 'Blame it on Breakfast' without the keyboards. Just to hear how it would sound, raw.

Owen is down on his knees in the middle of the small stage, his Nord keyboard balanced across two low pub stools, the laptop open behind it on a third stool. They lost the keyboard stand while they were loading up the van, or at least it hasn't made it to Galway with them. 'It'll sound stupid, that's how it'll sound,' he says, and Deirdre isn't in the mood for another row, so she gets him to come in on the last verse. She wishes she hadn't had the bright idea to bring her boyfriend on tour with her; she wishes that for one week she could be free from every kind of love.

*

Deirdre steps back into the venue and the song 'Horses' unfurls in her mind. When she first heard Patti Smith's voice, she decided she would become a singer, no matter what the nuns said. Life always comes back to the music, especially the music she loves. Eighties girl-pop (Banarama, The Bangles, Cyndi Lauper, The Go-Go's) and the depressive men (Tom Waits, Leonard Cohen, Nick Cave, Hank Williams, Vic Chestnutt). When she couldn't get enough of the kind of music she wanted to hear, songs started to write themselves in her head.

She can still smell the garlic on her breath from the cardboard pizza they ate after the sound check. She doesn't mind smelling of garlic, but when she is on the road surrounded by men in black T-shirts—hefting amplifiers and favourite guitars in and out of venues, testosterone on display wherever she turns—the strong odour leaking through her pores makes her feel like she is turning into one of them.

In the blank glare of the ladies' toilets, she pulls on her denim mini-skirt, the one she made out of an old pair of jeans an ex-boyfriend had left behind, and her superhero boots: calf-high blue boxing boots with deep red toes and bright yellow laces running all the way to the top. She leaves The Bangles T-shirt on; she figures she needs whatever moral support she can get, even if it is screen-printed.

Two minutes to nine o'clock and the venue is barren. It could probably fit a hundred-odd punters on a good night.

From the stage, the room looks even emptier. The black walls and floor suck in the light, so that the round wooden tables clustered in front of the stage seem to float up toward her. Tuesday Night Special at The Venue. Even the poster—she should have known her band would be bigger than the audience.

There are three of them sitting out there: Van, who drove them down here in spite of the cast on his right arm, Stephen her manager/ ex, and a teenage girl in a fifties-style dress who looks as if she must have a really good fake ID. She's the only one who scares Deirdre. She has been reading a book of poetry, which she carefully bookmarks and places beside her pint of Guinness the moment the band walks on stage. And Deirdre can see her lean forward out of the green shadow pooling around the pillar behind her, into the yellow lamplight that covers the front of the stage, her stage, the one she has just stepped onto, carefully picking her way around Eddie and his two back-up Telecasters, past Owen squatting down in front of a pub stool trying not to press the keys too hard in case the keyboard goes flying off its makeshift stand, and the tangle of cables Van and Stephen helped string around the stage, connecting each instrument to its amplifier, each amp to its power source, micing up every one of them—even John hiding behind his drums—so they can join her in the first chorus.

The room is still cold—only the spotlight gives her any heat—and the small round stools are still tidily gathered around the empty tables. She frets the note on the neck of her battered pale blue Danelectro bass.

Deirdre doesn't feel the sound.

John calls out time, and the band is off, playing without her. Deirdre tries to catch up, she's never missed an intro before, and when she should be singing her voice cracks. Stage death, and her life flashes in front of her eyes. Boyfriends, bills, too many different jobs, one shock pregnancy and one near-miss, pop soundtracks and Leonard's 'Hallelujah'.

She steps back from the microphone. 'Right, stop,' she calls and takes off her bass. She can't do it.

Deirdre knows this is the choice: sing now, to a near-empty room, for the one member of the audience who has paid the cover charge, or drop the bass guitar, let it break and go back to her temping data entry job, aim for permanence, a deposit for a house, singing in the shower, holidays and nice things because she is going to be thirty-five years old in March and this is not going to get any easier, the empty room and the stage alchemy.

'Give me three minutes.' But instead of charging off she stands in front of her microphone, whispers something that no one else can hear, and summons back her younger self—her shiny-eyed dreamer, the part of her that can do this gig—and summons back the music, the magic part of the world.

'Pass me your guitar,' she says to Eddie, and he hands it over, carefully, though he looks as though he would rather not.

Her voice relaxes open and she starts off unaccompanied on the opening lines of 'Bird on the Wire', the first song she ever learnt on the guitar. Then she goes for it—hammering out power chords on the borrowed guitar.

The music is taut. Deirdre's body is electric with what she sees when she looks out into the black room: the face of her daughter Lily—four years old and convinced she will one day rule the world—her own face at age four singing into a hairbrush, and at fourteen tearing her T-shirts, and at twenty-four with bright orange hair, ready to take on the world with music and poetry and the contents of her soul, and now she sings for the part of her that still chases butterflies around the balcony of their third-floor flat, for her little girl who thinks a song can make a midnight monster go away, she sings for the crap she has been through and the fed-up days yet to come, she sings as though her life depends on it.

Celeste Augé is an Irish-Canadian writer who has lived in Ireland since she was twelve years old, when her family moved from the backwoods of Northern Ontario, Canada. Over the years she has worked in various jobs—babysitter, waitress, shop assistant, library assistant, girl Friday, English literature tutor, community Writer-in-Residence—and now she teaches creative writing to adults and university undergraduates. When she was in her twenties, she dropped out of art college; in her thirties she completed an MA in Writing.

Her fiction and poetry have been widely published in literary journals and anthologies. Her poetry has been short-listed for a Hennessy Literary Award and Salmon Poetry have published her first full-length poetry collection, *The Essential Guide to Flight*. The Arts Council of Ireland awarded her a Literature Bursary. Her short story 'The Good Boat' won the 2011 Cúirt New Writing Prize for fiction.

She now lives in Connemara in the west of Ireland with her husband and son, a stone's throw from where her mother was born and reared.

Visit her website at www.celesteauge.com.
Contact her at cauge@eircom.net.